THE MIRACLE
MIND

Also by Sirshree

Spiritual Masterpieces - Self Realisation books for serious seekers

Who Am I Now: From mindfulness to no-mind
Answers that Awaken: Access the Source of Wisdom within You
100% Karma: Learn the Art of Conscious Karma that Liberates
100% Wisdom: Wisdom that leads you to experience and be established in your true nature
100% Meditation: Dip into the Stillness of Pure Awareness
You are Meditation: Discover Peace and Bliss Within
Essence of Devotion: From Devotee to Divinity
The Unshaken Mind: Discovering the Purpose, Power and Potential of your mind
The Supreme Quest: Your search for the Truth ends there where you are
The Greatest Freedom: Discover the key to an Awakened Living
Secret of The Third Side of The Coin: Unravelling Missing Links in Spirituality
Seek Forgiveness & be Free: Liberation from Karmic Bondage
Passwords to a Happy Life: The Art of Being Happy in all Situations

Self Help Treasures - Self Development books for success seekers

The Source of Health: The Key to Perfect Health Discovery
Inner Ninety Hidden Infinity: How to build your book of values
Inner 90 for Youth: The secret of reaching and staying at the peak of success
The Source for Youth: You have the power to change your life
Inner Magic: The Power of self-talk
Self Encounter: The Complete Path - Self Development to Self Realization
The Five Supreme Secrets of Life: Unveiling the Ways to Attain Wealth, Love and God
You are Not Lazy: A story of shifting from Laziness to Success
Freedom From Fear, Worry, Anger: How to be cool, calm and courageous
The Little Gita of Problem Solving: Gift of 18 Solutions to Any Problem
Freedom From Failure: 7 Spiritual Secrets That Transform Failure Into A Blessing

New Age Nuggets - Practical books on applied spirituality and self help

The Source: Power of Happy Thoughts
Secret of Happiness: Instant Happiness - Here and Now!
Excuse me God...: Fulfilling your wishes through the Power of Prayer and Seed of Faith
Help God to Help You: Whatever you do, do it with a smile
Ultimate Purpose of Success: Achieving Success in all five aspects of life
Celebrating Relationships: Bringing Love, Life, Laughter in Your Relations
Everything is a Game of Beliefs: Understanding is the Whole Thing
Detachment From Attachment: Gift of Freedom From Suffering
Emotional Freedom Through Spiritual Wisdom: How to Take Charge of Your Emotions

Profound Parables - Fiction books containing profound truths

Beyond Life: Conversations on Life After Death
The One Above: What if God was your neighbour?
The Warrior's Mirror: The Path To Peace
Master of Siddhartha: Revealing the Truth of Life and After-life
Put Stress to Rest: Utilizing Stress to Make Progress
The Source @ Work: A Story of Inspiration from Jeeodee

Author of the bestseller *The Source*
SIRSHREE

THE MIRACLE MIND

How to Master Your Mind
Before It Masters You

The Miracle Mind
How To Master Your Mind Before It Masters You
By Sirshree Tejparkhi

Copyright © Tejgyan Global Foundation
All Rights Reserved 2018

Tejgyan Global Foundation is a charitable organization
with its headquarters in Pune, India.

Published by WOW Publishings Pvt. Ltd., India

First edition published in July 2018

This book is based on the Hindi book, "Mann ka Vigyaan"

Copyrights are reserved with Tejgyan Global Foundation and publishing rights are vested exclusively with WOW Publishings Pvt. Ltd. This book is sold subject to the condition that it shall not by way of trade or otherwise, be lent, resold, hired out, or otherwise circulated without the publisher's prior written consent in any form of binding or cover other than that in which it is published and without a similar condition including this condition being imposed on the subsequent purchaser and without limiting the rights under copyright reserved above, no part of this publication may be reproduced, stored in or introduced into a retrieval system, or transmitted, in any form, or by any means, electronic, mechanical, photocopying, recording or otherwise, without the prior written permission of both the copyright owner and the above-mentioned publisher of this book. Any person who does any unauthorized act in relation to this publication may be liable to criminal prosecution and civil claims for damages.

*This book is dedicated to
the very first thought of the human mind,
with which the entire creation has come into existence
and also paved the way to master the mind*

How to get the best from this book

If you want to work upon your mind to attain mastery over it, this book will serve as a powerful and effective guide for you. Let's take a look at how this book is organized, so that you can make the most of it.

1. If you want to first get the basic understanding of the mind, you can begin from Chapter 1. If you already have knowledge about conscious, subconscious, and super-conscious mind, you can start reading from Chapter 2 onwards.
2. To identify negative habits of the mind and know about ways to overcome them, read Section II.
3. For learning the essential steps to become the master of your mind, read Section III.
4. To rise above entertainment and identify the actual goal of the mind, read Chapter 7 *'Freedom from the Dramas of the Mind.'*
5. If you have a restless mind, then to learn the lesson of patience, read Chapter 9 *'Training the Restless Mind to Overcome Delusion'*.
6. To attain freedom from vices of the mind, read Chapter 10 *'Improving the quality of the mind.'* It will be helpful to read this chapter several times to fully understand it and then implement the prescribed methods.
7. To get rid of tormenting thoughts, read Chapter 11 *'The Key to Self-introspection'* so that you come to know the actual producer and director of your thoughts.
8. To know how to deal with emotions arising in your mind and channelize them in the right direction, read Chapter 17 *'Emotional Maturity'*.

9. To understand different states as well as various vices and disorders of the mind, stories, analogies, and anecdotes have been extensively used in this book. By grasping their underlying meaning, you can gain the true understanding of the mind.

Contents

Preface   11

UNDERSTANDING THE MIND AND THE SECRET OF CHANGING ITS HABITS

1. Knowing the Mind   19
2. The Wrong Thinking of the Mind   31
3. Deformities of the Mind   37
4. The Secret of Freedom from Bad Habits   45
5. Entertainment - The Escape from Sorrow   53
6. Explosive Outbursts of the Mind   60
7. Freedom from the Dramas of the Mind   66
8. Attractions of the Mind and the Homepage   73

TECHNIQUES TO MASTER THE MIND

9. Training the Restless Mind to Overcome Delusion   81
10. Improving the Quality of the Mind   90

11. The Key to Self-Introspection	98
12. Power of Concentration	103
13. Getting Rid of Mental Impurities	109

HOW TO BE A MASTER OF YOUR MIND

14. Circumstances and the State Of Mind	119
15. Adopting a Learning Mindset	125
16. Yoga for the Mind	129
17. Emotional Maturity	135
18. Maintaining Right Focus	144
19. The Role of Difficulties in Life	151
20. Freedom from the Prison of the Ego	158

Preface

Kris wanted to perform a ritual of fire worship at home. He procured all the necessary items for the ritual. He also got an open tin box to be used as a cistern in which the sacrificial fire would be lit. He placed it in the courtyard of his house. Thereafter, Kris went out for some work.

After some time, a crow flew over the box, carrying a piece of meat in its beak. Somehow, the piece of meat slipped and fell inside the box. After a while, a man who was passing by, mistook the worship cistern to be a garbage bin and threw some old newspaper into it. Thereafter, several other people walking past also flung rubbish into it.

But the height of all these misunderstandings was when Kris himself wiped his hands with a tissue and tossed it into the box. He too had forgotten the very purpose of the box!

This anecdote has a deep message. It serves a reminder for each one of us to ask ourselves:

- Have I forgotten the purpose of my birth and indulged in "rubbish"?

- Due to lack of awareness, have I mistaken the worship-cistern of my mind to be a garbage bin, and filled it with the grime of hatred, malice, deceit, comparison, lies, greed, anger, and ego?

- Do I reflect on the truth that I have taken up this human form to transform my mind (which is a cistern for worship)?

- Have I realized that my mind is the greatest opportunity granted to me in my life?

Do these questions strike you? We have been born into this world to attain freedom from the exploits of the mind by understanding how the mind behaves and why. We are here to get rid of the mind's tendencies and hone its intrinsic powers to serve the higher cause of divine expression.

However, when we take an honest look within, many of us would find heaps of negative thoughts and emotions. Nobody or rarely few people attempt to clear this grime from the mind to make it pure and ever-blissful.

Consider a pond on a full-moon night with clear skies. If the pond is disturbed, it causes ripples due to which, the reflection of the moon shakes. This state of the pond symbolizes the agitated mind, which is infested with tendencies that bring suffering.

However, when the ripples are caused to settle and tendencies, which cause ripples, are also eliminated, the pond serves as a perfect mirror to reflect the resplendent full moon.

In the same way, the pure and unshakable mind serves as a brilliant expression of pure consciousness. It serves the very purpose of its creation, which is to manifest hitherto unknown creations on Earth. Such a mind can effect miracles in daily life. The word "miracle" has been associated with magic tricks or supernatural feats. But the miracle that the human mind is capable of, is beyond the realm of physical marvels.

The miracle mind makes the experience of life itself a miracle. It can lead you to a state where you revel in unbridled joy and unbroken peace. A miracle mind is open to the highest creativity, where ideas beyond the limits of the human intellect can be manifested. It is where the mind has learned to convert problems and seemingly sorrowful incidents into stepping stones for happiness and success.

The mind is the most valuable gift we have been given. It is the most powerful tool in the world, which we can use to attain the best and the highest possibilities in our life. However, without understanding the mind and how it works, every aspect of our life suffers. Our relationships deteriorate; we start feeling scarcity of love, peace, wealth, health, and happiness.

Once you understand your mind, it is indeed possible that the ever-changing mind would faithfully start obeying you. The miracle mind will always be happy, optimistic, enthusiastic, and give a devotional response to everyone. However, to attain such an exalted state of the mind, you need to give it the right direction and training. Only then can you become the master of your mind.

To become the master of your mind requires training your mind in such a manner that it remains peaceful or blissful in every situation. The journey of mastering the mind commences only when the mind remains steady, happy, and positive, despite problems, illnesses, or untoward incidents. This journey is nothing less than a pilgrimage; and this book will lead you on this pilgrimage. The outcome of this sacred journey would be a trained and pure mind.

The mind can understand everything that takes place on a laboratory table. But if we have to understand the mind itself, the mind has to be placed on the laboratory table. This requires a particular way of observation and contemplation.

In the external world, generally the mind gets trained by either circumstances or contemplation. Most people learn their lessons after they go through trials in their lives. However, the best way to train and master the mind is by changing its behavior through deep observation and contemplation.

This book lends the guidelines for observation and contemplation of the mind, which will bring the behavioral patterns and tendencies of the mind to light. The book reveals the facets of the mind that you should reflect on, and explains how you can direct your mind through reflection.

The greatest wonder of life is that there is something which is beyond your mind, which is your true essence. Once you discover this essence, your mind surrenders; wonders manifest. The mind emerges as the greatest opportunity only when it surrenders to that which is beyond it.

With the help of this book, you will be able to understand and transform the mind, which will make it unshakably peaceful, ever-enthusiastic, productive and at harmony with the world.

May you receive this greatest opportunity of life and may the supreme possibility of the human mind blossom within you. With this earnest intent, let's start reading this book...

SECTION I

UNDERSTANDING THE MIND
AND
THE SECRET OF CHANGING ITS HABITS

1

Knowing the Mind

The human mind has various aspects, functions, and forms. Thousands of thoughts pass through the mind every day, out of which very few are actually useful. The remaining useless thoughts can entangle the mind and drift it away or even lead it in an undesirable direction.

There was a famous poet who was also a philosopher and a scholarly orator. One night, he was reading the description of a palace. The palace was grand and opulent with magnificent fountains and gardens. The poet fell asleep while reading about this palace.

Though his conscious mind was asleep, his subconscious mind wasn't. He had a dream of the same palace that he was reading about. An exquisite poem about this palace occurred to him in his dream. He remembered the entire poem even on waking up. He immediately got up and started noting it down on a piece of paper.

Unfortunately, after just a few lines, someone came to meet him, which kept him busy for quite some time. Thereafter, he returned to his desk, but the poem had simply vanished from his memory. Try as he might, he couldn't recall it. The lines, which were already written felt so divine that he did not want to forcibly add anything to it. Thus, the poem remained incomplete.

Even though the erudite philosopher's mind was calm, yet he could not complete the beautiful poem just because of one distraction. Just like the individual who came to meet the poet diverted him, one stray thought can divert you; it can distract and upset your mind. The human mind, which is a storehouse of infinite power and innumerable secrets, can lead a helpless life on losing its direction.

The mind is a very powerful tool that we have received as a gift. But due to certain negative obstacles, it can deprive us of the greatest joy of life. Therefore, it is crucial to understand the mind, so as to give it a positive orientation.

What is the mind?

You may have come across various explanations of the mind from various sources. Some consider it to be a part of *akasha* (ether element or space), while others regard it as a part of Consciousness.

Some even consider the mind to be a sense organ. However, this sense organ is different from the rest. The objective of the mind is to control and operate the remaining senses.

Some philosophers have compared the mind with a coiled spring. Just like it's impossible to predict where the coiled spring will land once it is released, likewise, hardly anyone can predict when and where the mind will jump to.

Sometimes the mind has been compared to a wild elephant and sometimes to a monkey. However, the path to attain internal bliss also opens up with the help of the same mind. You can realize divinity with the help of the mind. When the mind surrenders, there is the possibility of realization of the Supreme Consciousness, the true Self, through the medium of the human body.

Where is the mind?

So, where is the mind located? You will agree that the mind is an invisible aspect, but its presence is constantly felt in the form of thoughts, just as breeze is invisble and yet felt by the movement of leaves.

Now if you are asked, "Where is your mind right now?" you might say, "It is present in this book through my eyes." This is because you are reading this book with the help of your eyes. However, in between, the mind did make a trip out of the book, as it pondered over the question, "Where is my mind right now?" The mind made that trip at such great speed that you didn't realize that it happened.

The mind travels at a tremendously high speed. That's why you cannot grasp it easily. In the spur of a moment, it can travel across the Earth to some other continent, and in the very next moment, it could reach your aching knees. You can read and understand 200 to 300 words in a minute, but the mind's speed is so much that it can conveniently listen to 800 words per minute. That is why it brings the remaining 500 words every minute in the form of either imagination of the future or thoughts of past events. This is the reason why many people cannot concentrate their mind.

How are thoughts related to the mind?

The mind can be likened to a sweater. If you pull out one thread of wool from a sweater and keep pulling it, eventually you will be left with just a heap of yarn. The sweater disappears; this means what you called as a "sweater" was only an illusion. Similarly, the mind is also an illusion, knitted with thoughts. When you allow your thoughts to arise and subside by witnessing them in a detached way, the mind disappears.

So, are thoughts and the mind two different entities? No, thoughts are like the string or thread of the mind. That is why the mind can also be called as a "bundle of thoughts." The reality is that all the thoughts along with the "I" thought constitute the mind. If there are no thoughts, the mind ceases to exist.

When there are no thoughts, inner silence prevails. This silence or stillness is always present, but is shrouded by thoughts. When thoughts disappear, this conscious silence is revealed. This silence is the experience of bliss and love. It is this silence, which exists beyond the mind, that we need to understand.

However, before that, we need to understand that the mind is merely a fabric made up of varied thoughts. Wherever your attention goes, thoughts begin to arise about that object. Suppose your attention goes to the garden. Your mind instantly reaches the garden and starts thinking about it. If your thoughts are gloomy, your mind feels miserable. Happy thoughts make your mind feel ecstatic.

At night when thoughts halt, we fall asleep. In the dream state, subtle thoughts become active for a short while. The mind is an instrument that weaves all these thoughts. In the waking state, thoughts run constantly. As soon as one thought culminates, another one arises. However, in the state of deep sleep, the series of thoughts comes to a standstill and we are in the state of thoughtlessness. We become thoughtless many times in the waking state too, but we don't realize it. This is because thoughts emerge one after the other at such great speed.

> Consider a man rushing to the railway station to take the train to his office. At that instant, his thoughts center around: "The train should arrive on time." Upon reaching the station, his thoughts turn to: "I must not miss the train." After boarding the train, he thinks: "Will I manage to get a seat for myself?" Once he is seated, his next thought is: "I should reach my office on time."

In this way, there is a perpetual stream of thoughts running in everyone's mind, and very few people get the thought that they should give a proper direction to their thoughts.

Different aspects of the mind

Generally, it is said that there are various types of minds. But, is it really so? The reality is that the mind has been given several names and categorized into various types simply for the sake of understanding its facets and functions. The purpose is to enable you to understand and utilize the faculties of the mind, instead of being enslaved by it.

The broad categories of the mind are the Conscious mind, the Subconscious mind, the Unconscious mind and the Super-conscious mind. Apart from these, the mind can also be categorized as the "Contrast mind" and the "Instinctive or

Simple mind". If all these types were to be classified into just two categories, that would be the "External mind" and the "Internal mind." Many different terms have been used only to understand these two minds in detail.

How the mind functions

You many wonder how all these facets of the mind fucntion in tandem. The scope of their work is immense. So, let's delve a bit deeper to understand the nature and functions of the Internal mind, the Simple mind, the Swinging mind, and the Contrast mind.

Internal mind

The Internal mind constitutes almost 90% of the entire mind. You may be aware that in an iceberg, only 10% of its volume is visible above water and the remaining 90% is submerged. In much the same manner, the Internal mind is present in a submerged state within you.

The difference between your External mind and Internal mind is the same as that between storm and air. The activity of the External mind is visible, whereas that of the Internal mind is not. The Internal mind operates your body automatically, without any effort from your side.

Imagine you are driving a car and all of a sudden a cyclist appears in your way. At that instant, you do not pause to think, "I should swerve to the right; but some children are playing over there. Ok, I'll swerve left; but there's a lot of sludge on that side and the tyres of my car may get caught in it. Fine, there's no option other than applying the brakes." No, you don't think all this; applying the brakes is an automatic response.

Later on, while narrating the incident, you might perhaps describe how you considered every aspect and then applied the brakes. The whole episode resurfaces from your memory and your External mind feels that it's the one that did it. However, ponder for a while to ascertain whether you really do it or it happens on its own? The automatic response is the function of your Internal mind.

Apart from that, various emotions like anger, frustration, guilt and resentment, are also suppressed in the Internal mind. We need liberation from these toxic suppressed emotions.

Simple mind

The Simple mind is a part of the External mind that is different from the Contrast mind but also uses the Internal mind. The Simple mind works according to the programming or conditioning of both the External mind and Internal mind. It is powered by the awareness of the External mind and the conditioning (memory and imagination) of the Internal mind.

The Simple mind acts as a bridge between the External and Internal mind. For example, when you are working on your computer, the Simple mind is operating and there are no other prevailing thoughts. Your only thought is of completing the task in the right manner.

When you drive a car, it's the Simple mind that directs you where to turn your car, or where to stop it. When you are totally engrossed in your work, the Simple mind is in action.

Swinging mind

The Swinging mind is the one that keeps oscillating and prattling between the past and the future.

When you were in school and Sundays were your day off, did you feel happier on Sundays or on Saturdays?

Most people would say that they were happier after returning from school on Saturdays. Now why's that so? Ideally, we should have been happier on the day off, i.e. Sunday, right?

The reason lies in the thoughts running in the mind. On Saturdays, most of us would gleefully think, "Tomorrow is Sunday… tomorrow is a holiday! Yay! It's going to be fun." However, on Sundays, we would be invaded by thoughts like: "Oh, tomorrow is Monday! It's back to school again. I have to complete my homework… and submit the assignment…"

This is the Swinging mind that dwells in the past or future, and in the process destroys the happiness of the present. It simply cannot stay in the current moment.

Contrast mind

When the mind is engrossed in comparison, judgment, jealousy, malice, and other negative thoughts, then it is known as the Contrast mind. The Contrast mind relishes feeling miserable by comparing oneself with others, or blindly running in the rat-race. It judges everyone and everything. It relentlessly categorizes every event you come across into two groups and labels them as good or bad, white or black; just like the contrast feature in the television. Your goal is to get rid of this facet of the mind.

Contrast mind Vs Simple mind

What's the difference between the Contrast mind and the Simple mind? Let's understand this with the help of an example.

When a painter is painting, his Simple mind is operating. While painting, his Simple mind thinks, "Let me see how this picture turns out." On the other hand, the Contrast mind thinks, "There is no value for paintings these days... What if someone's painting is better than mine? Would this picture sell or not? How much would it fetch?"

As soon as the Contrast mind becomes active, trouble begins. The Contrast mind dwells in a state of perpetual misery and suffering.

Various aspects of the Contrast mind

The Contrast mind is the manifestation of ignorance in human beings. It falls prey to several vices like comparison, lies, deceit, stress, ego, credit-taking (claiming credit for work that spontaneously happens), etc.

Have you ever heard of a sparrow committing suicide because it couldn't fly high like an eagle? Have you seen a peacock stressing because it couldn't fly like a flamingo? Or have you heard of an adult eagle refusing to teach a young one how to fly due to fear of being surpassed?

You may probably be wondering at the absurdity of these questions. You would be astonished to know that the art of living and the secret of true happiness are hidden in the answers of these questions. Real joy and the art of living have disappeared due to the act of comparison.

Generally, when people interact with each other, they either conceal, diminish, or exaggerate something to show off. When you listen to them, you may be easily carried away by their boasting and get stressed unnecessarily. Looking at their glamorous-appearing lifestyle, you may perhaps even give birth to the demon of jealousy within you. Sometimes, jealousy is so subtle and hidden that one easily fails to recognize its presence in the working of one's own mind.

Birds and animals do not have a contrast mind; hence they do not fall prey to comparison, stress, jealousy, or hatred. Humans possess the contrast mind and develop the habit of comparison, due to which they easily fall prey to numerous negative emotions. The habit of comparison is the strongest base for an unhappy mind. This habit becomes so deeply ingrained in the human psyche that it gradually turns into a monster, which works its destructive tendencies till the last day of life. Most people die with unhappiness due to this habit of comparison, without learning their life lessons.

The origin of comparison

When does the mind get afflicted with the habit of comparison? During childhood, this demon of comparison does not exist within us. It is frequently seen that when a sibling is born in the family, the older child is repeatedly compared with the younger one. One child is given less importance as compared to the one who fares well. This sows the seed of negativity in the mind of the aggrieved child.

On growing up, such children become easy victims of comparison. They start harboring the thought that they will never achieve anything significant in their lives. They suffer from self-loathing, inferiority and guilt. On the other hand, kids who are praised right from their childhood, are filled with ego and arrogance. In this way, both these kinds of children succumb to the ill-effects of comparison.

Method to conquer the mind

What is the difference between the mind and brain? The brain is a physical part of your body, whereas, the mind is invisible. If the mind reflects on a subject, the brain helps it with its intellectual faculty. For example, when you meditate upon a topic, you make use of your intellect. However, when thoughts are not in one direction, then the mind doesn't get to enjoy the company of the intellect. In that case, the mind becomes like a monkey that jumps in all directions.

Hence, first of all, one should protect one's intellect from being corrupted and going astray. Keep away from bad company. This means maintain a safe distance from people or objects that have a wrong influence on you. At a deeper level, this means, keep away from thoughts that have a wrong influence on you.

So, how can you enhance your intellect? Exercise your intellect by cultivating the habit of asking questions, such as: Where do we have to go and why? How to make this task easier? What is the need for this? Who are those great souls, who have traversed the path of attaining peace of mind and achieving mastery over their mind? What have they advised? Have they actually attained happiness by traversing this path or did they have to repent it? What is the ultimate purpose of my life? What is the difference between truth and untruth? The list can continue along this line.

In this way, the truth (essence) of life unfolds with the use of the intellect, guided by true wisdom. When the light of wisdom awakens in your intellect, it gives rise to *viveka*—the ability to distinguish between the truth and untruth. Without wisdom, the intellect remains weak and crippled and the mind turns into a monster.

When your intellect opens and blossoms, you begin self-enquiry: "Who am I? What is the cause of suffering? Does the cause of suffering reside within me? Why do we search outside for the cause of suffering?"

When this self-inquiry starts with *viveka*, the mind begins to calm down and the path to conquer your mind opens up.

2

The Wrong Thinking of the Mind

Once a man was travelling with his sister to a far off place. They checked into a hotel at night. While they were having a discussion in their room, their conversation was overheard by two businessmen staying in the adjacent room.

The discussion was about what should be done with the prince.

The sister asked, "How should we kill the prince? Should we stab him or poison him?"

The brother cautioned, "No, this is not the right time to kill the prince. We'll do it at a more suitable time. At present, he needs to be kept alive."

Both the businessmen were shocked on hearing this. They were certain that these people were hatching a plan to kill the prince of the state. Considering it to be their moral responsibility, they intimated the hotel manager about the ghastly plan, who immediately called the police.

The police arrived and arrested the accused. After a prolonged interrogation and a lot of hassle, it was learned that they had not been talking about the real prince. They were both novelists and were simply discussing the plot for their latest novel, in which the prince was a character.

The above incident is an example of how misunderstandings are created in our lives. Very often you don't know how the other person would interpret your statements. You speak with a certain intention, while the listener interprets it as something else. The same can happen when you are the listener too. As a result, there's every possibility of misunderstanding. Such situations deepen the roots of wrong notions or beliefs in the mind.

Meaning of wrong notions or beliefs

What exactly is meant by wrong notions or beliefs of the mind?

As a child grows, it learns to observe its surroundings, people, and events. At times, these observations create some illusions in his mind. If the child harbors these illusions even after growing up, then these are transformed into wrong beliefs or notions. Beliefs or notions are what your mind believes to be the truth, but aren't really so. Imagination regarding the shape, colour, and taste of an object are also notions. Let's understand this topic with the help of some examples.

The word "donut" automatically brings a ring-shaped object to your mind. One cannot think of a donut of any other shape, like a square or a cone. Similarly, the word "camera" usually brings a specific shape in mind. The reason is that the mind has been programmed in this manner, by observing the same shape of the specific object many times.

From the above examples, you may infer that your thoughts regarding a donut and a camera are right, because you too have seen those objects in those shapes numerous times in the past. However, the truth is that the shape of a donut or a camera can be totally different. But interestingly, the human mind only considers those attributes of the objects, environment, and people to be true that it has already seen and registered earlier.

Therefore, any such fixed ideas that the mind has considered to be true, are called notions or beliefs. In other words, any idea that is accepted without sufficient evidence is a wrong belief or notion.

Most people have several notions about their own capacity to work. For example, a person believes that he can work for only a certain number of hours a day, and not more than that. He feels that he simply cannot work beyond a certain point. These are self-imposed beliefs and not the truth.

The web of false beliefs

How does the web of false beliefs spread?

The mind considers these beliefs to be true, since everybody around it believes them to be so. When we see others strongly believing some idea, we too follow suit without question. Looking at us, our successors also start believing in them. In this way, the web of false beliefs keeps on expanding and flourishing.

If we are told that the number 13 or a black cat crossing our path are considered to be bad omens, we believe it and live with it, whereas, there remains no basis for such beliefs in our times.

Thoughts constantly keep arising in the human mind. Some of these thoughts give rise to certain fixed notions or beliefs. When these notions are examined to discern whether they are the truth, the reality becomes evident and we discover what the fact is, what the truth is, and what a false belief is.

The human mind is prone to form notions about every incident, situation, or individual that it comes across. For instance, the mind believes that it can perform certain tasks, and not some other tasks. At times, even before beginning a task, one doubts one's ability to complete it successfully. Due to such dilemmas, one is often unable to accomplish the decided task. As opposed to this, if the person has faith and is devoid of all such false beliefs, then every job becomes simple and easy for him.

Open up your closed mind, get rid of wrong thinking

What is the nature of false beliefs of the mind?

Let us consider another example to understand this.

> One day, a man cleaned his whole house. While cleaning, he came across a box which he wiped on the outside and placed back in the corner. He thought that since he had cleared every nook and corner, there wouldn't be a single cockroach left in his house. He was pleased to see the house spic and span. Suddenly, it struck him that the box which he had cleaned on its outside, should be opened and checked too. When he opened it, lo and behold! It was infested with cockroaches, which escaped from the confinement and started running everywhere in the house!

The human mind is also like this closed box, or rather a can of worms, filled with innumerable notions. When a person is asked to get rid of his false notions, initially he could be unaware that he's harboring so many notions in his mind. When the light of wisdom falls upon them, the notions start fading. It is then that the person realizes that there were numerous false beliefs present within him.

Get rid of false beliefs to enhance your abilities

How are your false beliefs related to your abilities?

Let's understand this with the example of a child.

> Once, a baby that was only a couple of months old, was thrown into water. Surprisingly, after struggling for a few moments initially, the baby started swimming. Despite the fact that the baby had no prior training in swimming, she was able to swim amazingly well.
>
> Imagine, if a grown-up person is sent to swim without prior training, what would he do? He would straightaway say, "I don't know how to swim; so then how can I do it?!"

This shows that we tend to weave a net of false beliefs about our abilities. What's also clear from this example is that the baby did not have any beliefs about the act or its ability to swim. On the other hand, the adult had various notions about swimming, which were enough to engulf him and hold him back. Neither the baby, nor the adult, were trained to swim. But just due to his preconceived notions, the grown-up person hesitated to even make an attempt to swim. The child was free from all such prejudices and could effortlessly swim. We live in the cocoon of our beliefs that limits the expression of our potential.

Freedom from beliefs with the help of logic

We can attain freedom from our limiting beliefs by identifying them and enhancing the quality of our mind. When the quality of the mind is raised, we can easily identify which of our thoughts are false beliefs and which ones are facts.

When we master the art of identifying our beliefs, we will be able to recognize our beliefs associated with every object, idea, environment, and people. And that's not all. We will also understand how and why these beliefs came into being in the first place.

At the same time, we also need to develop the habit of examining our thoughts against the framework of logic. With this, we will be able to distinguish between a fact and a notion. Otherwise, it is possible that we may often take wrong decisions on the basis of our wrong beliefs.

Therefore, before we accept others have concluded based on their judgment, we ought to validate it for ourselves first. For instance, people may say that it becomes difficult to learn something new, after a certain age. Before accepting this as the truth, we should attempt to learn something new after the specified age. We will find that there is no relation between learning and age.

We will understand that this statement is someone else's deduction, and not our own. We have to arrive at your own conclusions. To do that, we need to delve deep into the subject and unearth the truth of the matter as well as the falsity of our

3

Deformities of the Mind

After a lot of struggle, a young man somehow managed to get the job of a press reporter. One day, while rushing to attend an important meeting, he noticed a crowd by the side of the road. The young man thought, "Aha! Looks like someone has met with an accident. Let me go take a look. Whatever it is, it might turn out to be good for me. I may get a juicy piece of 'breaking news' from here."

He tried hard to get through the crowd to see what had happened, but he couldn't. Hence, he enquired with a person standing nearby, who said that there had been a major accident.

On hearing this, the young man got all the more excited. He intended to report this news immediately on reaching his office. But first, he had to see the accident scene and get the inside scoop. He once again attempted to penetrate the crowd, but when this proved to be rather difficult, he thought of an idea.

He started wailing. "Oh God! What have you done? You

took away my dear brother from me. How can I live without him?" He pushed the people around him and bellowed, "Get aside… at least let me see my brother."

On hearing his cries, people were taken aback and gave way to him. As soon as he saw the dead body, he was stunned and absolutely mortified. Everybody started laughing at him as it was a donkey that had met with an accident.

Many a times, an individual uses deceit and loses the trust that people have on him. He may gain the cooperation of others for some time, but loses respect as soon as the truth is revealed. As a result, he is unable to face anybody. Therefore, it's best to give up using deceit, pretentiousness and lies for gaining trivial benefits. Otherwise, all such wrong actions accumulate and one day, one has to pay a heavy price for them.

The major deformities of the mind

There are several deformities of the human mind. So, which deformity or flaw can you begin with, so as to begin the process of purifying your mind? You can begin with the eradication of deceit in your life. In the present age, this flaw is spreading deeper in the minds of people. In fact, it has such a far reaching effect that it is considered a skill rather than a defect these days. However, people do not realize that it is an act of self-deception.

In these times, as a student of a school or college, we acquire tons of information about the external world. Unfortunately, this information does not help us learn how to eliminate deceit and hypocrisy from our minds. Most people use the knowledge obtained through the education system to cater to their personal comforts and luxuries. In the modern education system, students are not trained to enhance the quality of their minds; instead, they learn the art of cleverly presenting the acquired information. More than developing core competence and living by principles, one is encouraged to develop superficial presentation skills, meant to impress the world.

It has become a common practice to alter or exaggerate facts during conversations. When youngsters in society observe grown-ups engaging in deceit, they too follow suit. As a result, they tend to spend more time in the world of fantasies, rather than the real world. In the long run, the habit of presenting a lie as a truth pushes individuals into the chasm of pretention, manipulation and despair.

The present society's structure is such that a deceitful person is termed "clever" or "smart", even though the person may be operating from greed. Such an individual does not hesitate to project a lie as the truth, just to impress his importance upon others. This fraudulent mentality causes more damage to one's own mind than anything else. Caught in the vices of the mind, people have turned into braggarts and bigmouths, instead of leading the mind on the path of true internal and external growth.

During conversations, most people misrepresent facts to gain praises and credit from others and feel so happy when they receive it. Such people live in an illusion as well as keep others in illusion. For instance, an individual narrates with great delight, "You won't believe what happened today! I cheated death. The situation was deadly, but I acted in such a smart manner that even death could not touch me."

However, consider whether the said situation was truly "deadly."

If it were indeed deadly, then is it really possible to outmaneuver death? If he is alive and kicking after encountering a lethal situation, then it is only due to the will of providence. However, an average person takes some steps and then feels happy to believe that he saved himself. Such mentality deteriorates the mind.

Cause of deterioration of the mind

What is the main cause of deterioration or decline of the mind? The habit of proclaiming all the credit for oneself gradually lands an individual in this state. Let's understand this in detail.

Generally, people tussle amongst themselves to take credit for any project that has proved to be a success. The person who has actually accomplished the job remains restless until he is given due credit. He waits impatiently to tell everyone that it was he who had done the job.

Craftiness of the mind increases further when the mind claims credit for even those jobs that it hasn't performed at all. If, by mistake, someone is given credit for a job that he hasn't performed, he doesn't decline it. The mind has this peculiar trait, it never attempts to clear such misconceptions. It thinks, "If people are mistaken, that's not my fault! So what if I'm given some credit?" This is the cunningness of the mind, arising from the seeds of dishonesty.

Even if an individual accomplishes a job using devious means, then too he gladly accepts all the credit and compliments for the job. In fact, he may believe that he fully deserves it for his "cleverness" and stamps his name on the job. Some individuals claim full credit even for work completed with the help of others, and use their power of persuasion to convince people that they are the ones responsible for the success of the job. On listening to them, people feel that these are smart individuals.

The crux of the matter is that most people try to claim credit even for tasks that are easily done. This "credit" is food for the ego. Therefore, it is essential to tell the mind clearly that any work is accomplished not because of the so-called smartness of the mind, but as a part of spontaneous happening by divine will. Even though the work is done through the body, the urge to do it is granted by divine providence.

When you feel upset on not being able to carry out a certain task in the expected manner, remind yourself that the divine will might wants to accomplish something better than that through you. This understanding will help you overcome sorrow and you would be ready to engage in new ventures.

When you complete a project as expected, and there is a hankering in your mind to get credit for it, remind yourself that even a leaf of a tree cannot shake without divine will. So, the entire credit goes to the Almighty. In this way, your mind would surrender and act in service to the divine will. Your external actions could appear the same, and yet it will be backed by this understanding of the truth.

If you want to make an elephant efficient in carrying heavy wooden logs, then you need to train it accordingly, so that it becomes capable of the task. On the other hand, if you wish that the elephant remains wild, you don't need to train it. It will remain wild by its nature. In the same way, to be able to control your mind, you need to train it. Your mind should be calm and restrained so that it would be capable of obeying your instructions. You also need to cleanse your mind.

For this to happen, examine your life with awareness and understanding, and ask yourself, "What do I achieve by claiming credit and what do I lose in doing so?" At your workplace, when credit brings you comforts and appreciation, you feel happy. However, it's not essential to always try to gain something; why not try living without credit for some time and see what happens? By doing so, you would be able to master your mind, and your mind would experience supreme happiness. This happiness is not dependent on any gain or cause, it is causeless. When you become a master of your mind, such inventions occur through you that bring about a new revolution in this world.

Eliminate deceit

What are the factors that drive a person to engage in deception? Fear, envy, attachment, ego, greed, etc. are the factors due to which an individual resorts to deceit.

> Once a woodcutter found a shining stone by the side of the dirt road. He picked up the stone and was looking at it, when a rich landlord happened to pass by. The landlord noticed the stone and immediately recognized it to be a diamond. Assuming the woodcutter to be ignorant, the landlord decided to strike a deal and usurp the diamond from him.
>
> "I will give you ten rupees for this shiny stone," he proposed. The woodcutter was not ready to part with the stone. The landlord raised his offer. "Fine. I shall give you 25 rupees and not a dime more. Now hand the stone over to me."
>
> "No, let me think for a while and then I'll decide whether to

give it to you," replied the woodcutter. "Ok. I will return to the village by this evening. By then you can decide what you want to do," said the landlord.

When the landlord returned to the village, he called on the woodcutter to know about his decision. The woodcutter told him that he had already sold it off for one hundred rupees. Hearing this, the landlord screamed, "You fool! What have you done? It wasn't an ordinary stone, it was a DIAMOND. It was worth thousands of rupees and you sold it off at the price of peanuts!"

The woodcutter laughed, "I haven't sold it yet. I wanted to find its actual price and so I lied to you, so as to get the true price out of you."

These are the kinds of deception that the mind indulges in, which often appear to be true. What is the understanding that the mind should be given so that it can leave its tendency of deception?

We need to always remain aware so that neither can others deceive us, nor would we try to deceive others. Even if a situation arises, we need to ask ourselves whether we really need to manipulate the truth.

In the above example, the landlord thought he was very clever, but the illiterate woodcutter was able to catch his deception by engaging in deceit himself!

There are people who lie even when there's no need to. On top of that, they think they did good and expect to be applauded for it.

Very often people think, "What's the harm if I indulge in a little deceit? Nobody would even come to know about it." But they forget that nature's system is foolproof. It's the law of nature that whatever you give, returns to you manifold. Be it good or bad, honesty or dishonesty, truth or falsehood. Therefore, it's wise to give up the habit of exaggerating or hiding the truth, and instead learn the workings of the mind.

4

The Secret of Freedom From Bad Habits

There was a rich man who entrusted a wise old man with the responsibility of getting his young son rid of his bad habits.

The old man invited the young man to a garden for a stroll. During their stroll, the old man asked the young man to uproot a small plant. The young man easily ripped it out. On walking a bit further, the old man asked him to pull out a bigger bush. The young man managed to do that too.

After a while, the old man asked him to uproot a full grown guava tree. In spite of applying all his strength, the young man could not pull out the tree and gave up saying it wasn't possible for him. The old man took this opportunity to explain some things to the young man. He said, "It's the same with our wrong habits. When wrong habits are allowed to stay and grow, they become deeply rooted and turn into stubborn habits. Then it becomes impossible to uproot them. Therefore, it's always better to nip them in the bud."

This little story clearly indicates that you have to struggle to remove bad habits that have grown with time. As rightly said: Old habits die hard.

People who smoke or drink caffeine find it very difficult to give up these habits. They are of the opinion that if they don't smoke or drink caffeine, they would be edgy and irritated the whole day and won't be able to function well. Due to this misconception, many people begin their day's work only after having a drink. The habit of drinking is so deeply ingrained in some people that if they don't drink, they feel agitated.

Bad habits are not limited to physical ones but include mental ones as well. There are many women who indulge in backbiting and gossip and find it very difficult to give up that habit. The effect of this habit is so deep that not only are their conversations filled with slander, but even when alone, the thoughts going on in their minds are filled with spite. They get restless within a short time if they don't badmouth about someone.

It's a serious symptom if you feel uneasy about not indulging in a habit. In other words, if you simply cannot do without it, then it's a dangerous sign. It is crucial to work on overcoming that habit well in time. To do so, firstly identify all the alarming signs. Secondly, give your mind this message repeatedly: "It is possible to lead a healthy, normal, and powerful life without succumbing to such habits." Thirdly, try various experiments to get rid of the habit. Your self-confidence will rise with these experiments. At the same time, always remember that habits are meant to make your life better and not to convert you into a slave to them.

Bad habits and mental programming

How exactly do bad habits operate? A bad habit acts as a blindfold, due to which you stop seeing its harmful effects. This strengthens the hold of this habit on you and subsequently it develops a trigger-point in your brain. You may not know how to eliminate these trigger-points from your brain. With the passage of time, it becomes difficult to free yourself from the clutches of that habit, since by then it has been deeply embedded in your brain.

For example, when the habit of drinking alcohol is deeply entrenched, it's difficult to get rid of it. Even if one wants to get rid of it, the trigger-points in the brain do not allow that. One feels like drinking as soon as one gets the chance. Besides drinking, there are many other habits which an individual cannot give up even if he wants to. He is tempted by the mere thought of them. For example, most people salivate on the mere mention of pickles.

This is what happens with those women too, who cannot quit binge-shopping or backbiting, despite genuine efforts. The trigger-points present in their minds don't let them and that's why they remain addicted to those habits for years together.

To achieve freedom from these wrong habits, first and foremost, raise your level of awareness to find out which trigger-points are causing you to indulge time and again. When you can clearly see the futility of these habits and the harm they cause, these bad habits will automatically start dropping off like dead skin.

For example, if a frog is placed in a pot of boiling water, it jumps out at once. However, if the same frog is kept in a pot of cold water, and the water is slowly heated, the frog gets accustomed to staying in it; though eventually it might even die in the scalding water. The same thing applies to our bad habits. We should kick them off before they weaken us or even kill us.

Surprisingly, many of us don't develop any affinity for good habits. Most of us don't find a glass of bittergourd juice or a bowl of boiled vegetables tempting. On the other hand, we can hardly resist crispy, fried, or spicy food. Therefore, we need to be extra intent and fervent to cultivate good habits.

Releasing negative habits and adopting positive ones are two sides of the same coin. If you are asked to work on any one of them, then your focus should be on 'adopting' something and not on 'releasing.' Focus your attention on positive habits.

How to change the habits of the mind

How to control the mind that is generally prone to inertia and irritable? Many a time, you have to work really hard to change your habits because the mind tends to revert to its old habits again and again. At such times, consider this struggle as a test for life and stick to the new, positive habits.

A discerning human mind knows very well that it has certain unwanted habits that need to be relinquished. To achieve that, it needs to take a positive turn. For example, if you want to get rid of anger, you have to practice meditation regularly and cultivate the habit of remaining calm in the face of irking situations. As a result of meditation, you would gradually realize that anger is causing harm to you as well as to others. Further, you would comprehend that it cannot be guaranteed that your anger would yield positive results. For instance, if a dad gets angry with his son for keeping the lights on for a long time without any reason, then it cannot be said for certain that the son would immediately switch off the lights next time. It's quite possible that his dad's anger might make him more negative and stubborn.

When you deeply contemplate the deformities of your mind, your false beliefs, wrong notions, and the events taking place around you, you will then be able to grasp their futility. When you react under the influence of these deformities, you are the first one to become a victim of such an action. With this perspective, try your best to adopt new and constructive habits.

Most of us know that daily exercise and *pranayama* in the morning are good for our health. However, out of sheer laziness, most people fail to follow this routine. Later on, when they are afflicted by some disease, they are compelled to think, "Why am I so careless about my physical wellbeing? Where is my laziness leading me? How can I gain and maintain good health by continuing this lifestyle?" When you answer these questions honestly, that's when positive changes begin in your life.

One who is honest to oneself progresses in life. There are several people who don't exercise due to lethargy and waste their golden morning hours. As a result, they spend the whole day under stress. This adversely affects their physical health in the long run. Some of them even reach the hospital and some even get admitted in the Intensive Care Unit. Then they need to begin with medicines and exercises to regain their health. To avert a substantial and possibly irreversible loss, one must change their wrong habits through contemplation while the body is healthy.

Physical health and mental habits

What is the relationship between physical health and mental habits? There is an intimate connection between the body and mind. Physical tension can affect your mind, due to which it feels depressed. On the other hand, mental stress can affect your body, making it tired and weak. In this way, both the mind and body affect each other. If you work on getting rid of your mental habits, you will achieve freedom from physical vices too. Let's understand this with the help of some examples.

> There was a man who was addicted to drinking several cups of tea every day. One day he developed severe hyperacidity and suffered from its agonizing symptoms. That day, he vowed never to drink tea again in his life, because he realized his physical wellbeing was far more important than the taste of tea. This helped him get rid of his addiction.

> There was another man who was very fond of sweets. Whenever he had the urge for it, he would pop 3 to 4 pieces in his mouth. One day he developed an unbearable stomach ache. When this pain recurred a couple of times, he honestly pondered upon the reason and found that consuming excessive sweets was the main cause. When this came to light, he gradually reduced his sweet intake and then stopped it altogether.

Each person has to individually reflect upon their physical and mental tendencies, and change them accordingly. Honesty and reflection are vital to overcome greed, impatience, attachment, and so forth. This enables you to progress on the path of growth. When your bad habits give way to good habits, you grow in every aspect of your life. When one is unable to bring that change, then one repeatedly slips when faced with testing situations.

One day, a man was walking down the street and stepped on a banana peel, which he had failed to notice. He slipped and fell. Fortunately, it did not cause any injury.

The next day, he actually noticed a banana peel on the sidewalk. He said, "Oh dear! Not again! I'll have to slip and fall again today." He stepped on it and fell down.

The third day, on the same path, he noticed two banana peels lying some distance apart. Now he was in a dilemma. "Which peel should I step on, the right one, or the left?"

The above scenario may seem funny, but much in the same manner, when we are enslaved by bad habits, we repeat the same mistakes again and again. It's time to free ourselves from this rigmarole.

Give a positive direction to your mind by repeating the affirmations given below. You will see their effect increasing day by day. These affirmations will endow you with physical health, which will in turn keep you mentally fit too. Your words have power. They can actualize and manifest in your life. Hence, always use positive and powerful words. Apart from this, note down some inspirational positive lines in your diary and repeat them often to get rid of diseases and negative habits.

- ◆ The illness or habit that is no longer required by me is leaving my body and mind.

- My body is once again producing all the secretions and hormones required for good health[#] and my mind is also becoming pure.

- I always feel young and energetic. My mind has become a treasure trove of happiness.

- I am getting better and I feel fully healthy. My body and mind are filled with abundant energy.

- If there is any disease present in my body or mind, it is getting cured speedily and completely.

- With every passing day, my mind and body are getting better.

- I am God's property. No illness or negativity can harm my body or mind.

[#] For understanding the principles and techniques to attain complete health, you may read the book, **"The Source of Health"** by Sirshree.

5

Entertainment – The Escape From Sorrow

A man developed a very painful boil on his body and visited a clinic for its treatment. During examination, when the doctor was going to touch the affected area, the boil called out, "Oh Doctor! Please don't touch me. It's very painful." The doctor was taken aback. First of all, how could a boil speak? Secondly, if he couldn't examine it, how would he prescribe a remedy?

If the disease itself instructs the doctor not to touch it and how to go about the treatment, it would be so difficult for doctors to do their job. If the disease begins to dictate terms, that would be the biggest disease!

This hypothetical example shows how a human mind, just like the boil, speaks as if its cure is not possible. We are so deeply attached to our mind that we obey whatever it says. Due to this, mental ailments like depression, confusion, lethargy, and other mental disorders perpetually survive without being noticed.

Attitude of a sad and diseased mind

How does a sad and ill mind behave and how should it be treated? Physical ailments and their treatment are a natural course of life. When one develops a physical illness, finding its cure becomes the first priority. Surprisingly, it has never been the same for mental illnesses.

Most of us take the treatment of physical ailments with utmost seriousness, whereas we tend to neglect mental ailments with equal carelessness. One of the reasons for neglecting mental disease is that it is not as tangible or evident as physical disease. This is why there have been very less discoveries and inventions in the domain of mental diseases as compared to physical diseases. There are many aspects of the human mind which are still unknown to us; and the reason for this is the wrong behavior and chatter of the mind.

Wrong interpretations and declarations by the mind only makes a mess of things. An unhappy mind often deplores, "Nobody in this world must have faced the amount of suffering that I've undergone!" And then, in an attempt to look for a solution to this despair, an individual may narrate his sorrow to all and sundry. In this process, all his words spoken with such emotion actualize and manifest in his life. This multiplies his sorrows. The direct remedy for this is: Do not pour your heart out to one and all.

Habit of entertainment

People have discovered entertainment as the most convenient method to escape misery. Everybody finds it easier to indulge in entertainment instead of encountering the painful thoughts arising in their minds. This is the reason why so many modes of entertainment are available today. People don't even realize how 2 to 3 hours of theiri precious time can easily slip away while watching a movie. The height is when people feel proud about watching the same movie several times!

The whole world today seems to be in agreement that the unhappy mind should be engaged in entertainment, so that it would stop troubling you and remain calm for some time. You can enjoy entertainment as long as you have good health. When the body stops supporting you, you can take it as the warning bells to wake up. You can work on your mind at that time too, but many people fail to take that opportunity as well.

Entertainment of the mind also includes the habit of blaming and ridiculing others. Mocking a disliked family member also happens to be a favorite past time of many.

The need for entertainment

Why has the need for entertainment risen to such an extent? Humorous poems and jokes were invented as a means of delight; however, today the situation is such that people believe if they don't indulge in this cheap and obscene entertainment, it will make their lives insipid. That's why the need for such entertainment has escalated so much that people are unable to live without it. As a result of such dependency, people become prone to emotional disorders. However, with a little awareness, they can mend themselves.

After the day's work, the first thought that comes to mind is: *I have worked a lot today, so now I deserve entertainment in order to relax and chill.* The popular modes of entertainment that a person indulges in are WhatsApp or Facebook or games on mobile phones, watching their favorite TV shows, or relishing their favorite dishes. If you spend such free time reflecting on your entire day's activities, you'd may perhaps find that you have rarely peacefully connected with your true inner self.

You *can* stay connected with your inner self while performing your day to day activities. But non-awareness, ignorance, and misery spur you into such activities which reduce the possibility of your inner awakening. Consequently, your problems multiply and you remain busy solving them throughout your life. Your life could have been easy, simple, and powerful; but instead it becomes ignorant, complicated and lacking awareness.

For instance, a person boasts of having plenty of money, which he says he has lent to a friend, who's going to repay him. In the meantime, he needs to borrow some amount. Some people believe him and lend him money. In this way, he is able to deceive others with his tricks and get benefitted for some time. He mistakenly considers this to be God's grace. However, when he repeatedly indulges in this sham, and one day faces grave consequences, he realizes that what he considered 'grace' was actually his 'ignorance.' One should awaken and get rid of deceit before any irreparable damage occurs.

There are others who feel quite satisfied with the comforts and luxuries that they have attained in their lives. They say, "We have achieved everything that we wanted to. We don't need any wisdom or spiritual knowledge. Our children need it; let them learn." Their basic necessities of life have been fulfilled; they have come out of the pits or struggle and are now walking on the smooth road. However, they haven't reached their destination. The difference between these people and children is that children are still digging new pits, whereas these people have come out of the old pits on the road. Yet, both are yet to achieve the ultimate goal of this earthly life.

The ultimate goal of our life on Earth is to be established in our true inner self, and lead our lives as the infinite divine self. This is the royal path. Those who walk this path are able to get rid of all the flaws of the mind and attain the supreme truth by abiding in divine love, bliss, and devotion. Else, people remain immersed in the entertainment of this illusory world and the dramas of the mind to such an extent that they fall in love with it. They get attached to the body to such an extent that they remain immersed in the dramas of this world.

States of mind and inner experience of the Self

You can indeed attain freedom from sorrow and entertainment by understanding the various states of the mind. To make this happen, whenever an unhappy emotion arises in the mind, ask yourself, "Am I feeling sad, glad, mad, afraid, or dead at this time?"

Sad includes the state of misery and worry.

Glad includes all happy and joyful states.

Mad includes the state of displeasure and anger.

Afraid comprises fear of illness or death and any other fears with regards to yourself and your near and dear ones.

Dead implies the state of numbness in which the mind cannot understand anything.

If you are experiencing any of these mental states, it indicates that you are disconnected from your true inner self, which is always peaceful and blissful. If that's the case, examine the state of your mind, remind yourself that you are not the mind, detach yourself from it, and reconnect to your true self to experience peace and joy.

You have to believe that there is nothing and no one in this world who can prevent you from attaining everlasting happiness. It's you who keep holding yourself back from abiding in that state of unbroken bliss within you. That bliss is always trying to pull you towards it. So, whenever any negative state of the mind tries to overwhelm you, become aware of the pull from your inner bliss and consciously move towards it.

Freedom from double sorrow

When does sorrow increase and what should your mind be taught, so as to overcome it? When you try to find a solution to your problems with negative emotions filled in your mind, that's when your problems and sorrows increase. After that, you may feel unhappy about your sorrow too. Sorrow over sorrow – this is double-sorrow.

For example, if a person has a physical pain, then he suffers it and to add to it, he feels miserable about having that pain too. This is pain over pain, or double pain. He keeps thinking, "How long is this pain going to continue? Why do I have to suffer? Why me?! Why me?"

In such cases, the mind should be given the understanding that it's okay to have pain, but there is no need to harbor pain about the pain. It's okay to have sorrow, but not sorrow about the sorrow.

The cycle of joy and sorrow is always going on in nature. Your mind suffers from double sorrow when sorrow appears in your life, but it also suffers when joy disappears. Therefore, you need to learn to look at joy and sorrow from the right perspective and discover the secret of life, beyond this duality of opposites.

6

Explosive Outbursts of the Mind

At the end of the class, the teacher announced, "There will be a lunar eclipse at 8 o' clock tonight. Don't forget to watch the event."

A student promptly asked, "Sir, on which TV channel can we watch it?"

From the student's response, you can easily understand why the thought of watching the eclipse on TV occurred to him. That's because today, everyone is so habituated to entertainment and a luxurious lifestyle that these are considered to be permanent solutions to boredom.

By constantly using television, the Internet, mobile phones, and other gadgets, people are becoming slaves of their minds. It is necessary to ponder for a while: how many hours do we spend aimlessly being glued onto the television or the mobile phone, which has led to dramas and outbursts in our lives?

Explosion of the mind

Does the human mind explode like a bomb? Let's understand this with an anecdote.

> A man was travelling by bus. He was carrying a big parcel in his hands and was lost in thoughts. After a while, the conductor of the bus noticed and inquired what the parcel contained. The man said, "It contains a bomb." Even after hearing this, the conductor did not get perturbed. He asked, "Where are you taking it?" The passenger replied, "I found it at this particular place and am now taking it to the police." The conductor advised, "You can keep it beneath your seat and then sit comfortably."
>
> The passenger complied with the conductor's suggestion and heaved a sigh of relief, as if he was now free from the danger of the bomb. But we can see that he wasn't actually free from the danger because the bomb could explode anytime and claim the lives of all the people travelling in that bus. What was needed was to diffuse the bomb.

In this anecdote, the bomb symbolizes the human mind. The unrestrained thoughts of the mind cause fear or sorrow and create attachment. Negative thoughts can mislead one to such an extent that he may put his own life or someone else's at stake. If the mind becomes dominant, a person can even kill someone. The root cause of so many atrocities in the world today lies in the mind which is filled with ignorance and negative thoughts.

Today, almost everyone is carrying a bomb (read "mind" here) that can explode (lose control) any moment. This is why everyone needs to learn the art of diffusing this mental bomb. To learn this art, you should first be able to identify the dramas your mind plays at the various stages of your life.

Childhood dramas

When do the dramas of the mind begin? When a child is barely two or two-and-a-half years old, the tendency of playing dramas takes root in the mind. To get an object of its liking, the child's mind either resorts to crying and screaming or makes a grumpy face and feigns displeasure. When the child approaches his parents with puppy dog eyes and an innocent face, the parents cannot resist asking him what he wants. At that time, if a guest happens to visit and sees the innocent look of the child, the guest too says that the child should be given whatever he or she wants. By achieving success in this way, the child gets the first lesson on drama.

Some children feign stomach pain when they don't want to go to school. They clutch their stomach and start crying. Believing them, mothers allow them to stay home. Thus, the children get the desired result with their pretensions.

A small child is not strong enough to carry out all its activities on its own. In fact, it is dependent on others for every little thing, like opening the wrapper of a candy, taking out a toy from the cupboard, or opening the door to go out to play. To get all these things done, the child resorts to dramas, which in due course develops into a habit.

Bigger dramas of grown-up minds

We have seen that a child manages to get things done by pretending and feigning. Unfortunately, even on growing up, they continue with such dramas. The underlying desire is: "I should get what I want; people should give me love and attention; this particular thing should get done; I should get some convenience or rest; people must listen to me, understand me, respect me," etc. The mind keeps engaging in dramas to fulfil all its wishes, however childish they may be.

Generally, people want others to comply with them and do what they want them to do, be it in the family or at the workplace. If they don't see that happening, they don't desist from creating drama or throwing tantrums. By creating a different drama every time, these dramas become a part of them to such an extent that they are unable to separate themselves from those pretenses. The biggest loss is that they move away from their true self, and never introspect to realize what they are losing due to such theatrics.

Now it's time for you to reflect in retrospect: Which dramas did you play in your childhood and why? Also, what was the ultimate result of those dramas? Did those dramas work or not? When a person experiences failure in any aspect, it becomes an opportunity for introspecting and finding the cause of failure, which then helps him in giving up wrong practices and moving on the right path of progress.

Otherwise, if he always succeeds by using his tricks, he would never contemplate his actions and find the truth that he's needlessly performing wrong karma. In other words, if all the dramas were successful, then the individual would lead one's entire life as a drama artist.

The games played by men and women are different, as they are constitutionally different in nature. Many a times, when a lady needs a household item for the family, she usually may not ask for it directly, but might be disgruntled and hint at it indirectly. For instance, the requirement of a new refrigerator would be placed as, "There's simply no space in this fridge! I have to somehow shove everything in it. When I open its door, everything falls out. This is disgusting!" One has to take the cue that a bigger refrigerator needs to be bought at the earliest.

There are women who feign headache when they have guests. They carry out the household chores, wearing a band around their head so that when guests would advise them to rest, they can express their inability to do so, due to *so much work*. Gaining sympathy from the guests is their ulterior objective.

In the same manner, there are men who at times, twist the facts a bit to make the situation light. There is no harm with that. However, when men twist facts in order to throw their weight around or to control others, then those actions are harmful theatrics of the mind.

Children use various tactics to achieve their object of desire. They continue with their ploys without bothering what others would think of them. However, adults are very much concerned about their own image, and that's why their pretensions are more sophisticated and not easily detected.

Many people play out dramas to gain extra love, care and attention from others. However, upon attaining spiritual wisdom, they realize that there is no need to hanker for love, because the source of love resides within them. Those who have realized and experienced their inner self don't need to get entangled in such exploits of the mind.

The body-mind is a mirror

If the act of entertainment is performed for the enjoyment of the mind, then why does the mind get entangled in it? Everywhere in this world, artists perform plays on stage. Their basic objective is to entertain the spectators' minds for some time. However, here we are not discussing an external stage, but the drama being played on the stage created by God himself – this world. When a person gets entangled in this play, then begins the drama of the mind.

The reality is that the formless and limitless 'Self' or consciousness is associated with the human body-mind only to experience itself and express its divine qualities. The body-mind has been created merely as a mirror to experience our true Self. Unfortunately, the Self has got entangled in the world of its own creation and forgotten to look into the mirror to experience its true nature.

It is time for us to understand this fundamental objective of the drama of life being played out on Earth and enjoy it, rather than getting stuck in the drama and wasting the entire life.

7

Freedom from the Dramas of the Mind

Those, who get caught up in the pretensions of the mind, find it hard to overcome them. Some keep struggling for their entire life, and yet do not succeed. Therefore, one must know the importance of always remaining alert and aware in life and learn the art of diffusing the mental bomb, well in time.

How to diffuse the mental bomb

One can diffuse the mental bomb by providing the right direction to the mind. During your school days, you received the required directions from your teachers. At the workplace, your boss decides your professional goals. In the family, the couple together decide the short-term and long-term objectives for the family. In all these cases, you do not have a personal objective. Now is the time for you to provide a strong and practical objective to your mind, so that, this very mind becomes the source of your happiness.

There are several quick means of temptation available these days to relieve the mind of its tensions. Some are of the opinion that the mental bomb need to be shoved under the seat. In other words, the widespread solution is to keep the mind constantly engaged in entertainment.

Entertainment is only a means to provide a momentary relief to the taxed mind. It is only a temporary escape from the vexed mind; it cannot diffuse the mental bomb. On the contrary, with indiscriminate indulgence in entertainment, the chances of explosion of the mental bomb increase. The mind gets attuned to whatever it is fed. Too much of entertainment makes the mind resonate at the level of the content that it dwells in. As a result, the outbursts of the mind increase.

If you ponder for a while, you would know that people have been advised in many different ways to overcome the whims of the mind. People come up with various complaints: I am in great trouble, I feel troubled by the demands of my family, my partner doesn't cooperate, my colleagues are non-supportive, etc. Such people are misguided by priests, who convince them that their problems can be alleviated if they were to make an offering to a particular temple, or wear an amulet on the arm, and so on. And surprisingly, people believe in them, too.

On the demise of a near one, the priests advise the family members of the deceased to conduct some rituals. They are told that the deceased soul would get to heaven and attain liberation if these rituals are followed. Due to sheer ignorance, many people even consider these advices to be effective and perform them accordingly. These priests, who advocate rituals, are always ready with solutions to all kinds of problems. People blindly follow their advices without even questioning them once. This is the example of a mental bomb which a person carries with him even to the place of worship – be it a temple, a mosque, or a church. It is indeed surprising that the person who wants to get rid of his mental fancies carries his mind with him wherever he goes in the journey of life, just like the passenger from the previous chapter, who wants to get rid of the bomb, but carries it with him on his trip.

The relationship between mind, body and emotions

In everyday life, each person goes through incidents that trigger pleasurable or painful emotions within them. These emotions, when not dealt with properly, leave indelible impressions in his body. They remain in the body memory and resurface when similar episodes recur. These impressions then get triggered and emerge as fear, anger, dislike, greed, hatred, malice etc.

As soon as negative emotions takeover, the person experiences a burden and the experience of his true self becomes blurred. In such situations, he must witness the emotions with alertness and forbearance. If done so, there is a possibility that he would not get driven by his emotions. When the emotions that arise are witnessed without being drawn into their play, they also get released from the body.

Shifting from the drama to the true self

How should we regard the play of the mind? The first truth that we should realize is that we are not just thinking machines. We are not our minds. Rather, the thinking machine is an instrument that we use. Upon careful observation, we will find that we are not our bodies, since we can observe, sense and feel our bodies. Whatever is being observed is not the observer.

Even our thoughts can be observed. We can take some time out to observe our thoughts as they arise and subside. As we practice this, we find that we are not our thoughts. We are the knower of our thoughts, the knower of our mind. This knowing continues to exist even in the gap between thoughts.

This deep knowing or consciousness is the essence of life. It is the Source of life. Everything arises from this Source. It is who we truly are – beyond the body and mind. Consciousness can be experienced as the feeling of beingness, of being alive and awake to whatever is happening. This song of beingness is being played constantly; we are that song! Being aware of this song gives the experience of pure joy, unconditional and boundless, independent of the world, untouched by situations.

When you identify with this consciousness as the real "I", you gain a new perspective of the mental dramas being staged on this screen of consciousness. From this standpoint, it becomes easy to detach from the drama and remain untouched by it. You decide not to be involved in the pretensions and illusions of the mind, but to remain rooted in awareness of who-you-truly-are. Recognition of your true nature as pure consciousness automatically leads to such a resolution.

This resolution keeps you alert. Then you can gain a clear view of the fancies of your mind and their outcome. You can understand that these mental fancies are only entangling and diverting you from your real purpose. With alertness and clear vision, it is possible to emerge from the web of mental filters and limiting beliefs.

The ultimate purpose of life can be attained only when one gains conviction that who-one-truly-is is separate from the body and mind. When one learns to watch the play of the body and mind in a detached manner from a standpoint of equanimity, one gains the conviction that "I am not this body; nor am I this mind." The Self gets associated with the body-mind only to realize its own nature and express its divine qualities. Therefore, to live in this world, the Self should be attached to the body and mind only as much as it is necessary to experience and express itself. This art is to be learnt while living in this world.

As the lotus blossoms in mud but is not sullied by it, so can the Self remain in this world, untarnished. You can connect with your body from the standpoint of the essential experience of who-you-truly-are. In the context of connecting with the world, when you are working together with others, you should get attached to people only to the extent needed to fulfil your role, and not more than that.

While playing his part in this world-stage, one should remember that he is actually the Self, beyond body and mind; and he is only playing his role by being associated with this body. It is important to remember "who am I" when one is not playing the role. It is essential to be detached from this body-mind and its myriad roles to return to the experience of one's true Self.

However, just the opposite happens here. When the person is applauded for his exquisite acting, they get elated, over-act and in the process, assume the play to be true. Thus, one begins by pretending to be the role one plays, and by indulging in these pretentions, one forgets that one is pretending. One becomes the role and finds it difficult to return to the essential experience of the true Self.

For example, when an actor plays the role of a specific character for a very long time, he becomes identified with the character to such an extent, that he considers it to be true. This has been found to be the case with several artists in the world of movies and entertainment. There have been actors who played so many tragedy roles that depression became an intrinsic part of their personality. Doctors had to ultimately advise them to take up some comic roles to come out of this syndrome.

Similarly, there are actors who get so engrossed with their roles that they consider their characters to be the real ones. Those who become renowned are more prone to this threat. Gradually, they get accustomed to the drama, thinking it was their need, completely forgetting that the drama was meant for mere entertainment. When one remembers this fact, then it is possible to enjoy the fancies of the mind while remaining aloof from them.

To make this happen, one has to keep aside a specific time for meditation in one's daily routine. Meditation is a state wherein you can go beyond the sense of the body and mind and enter a state of pure conscious being, beyond thoughts. This state is the experience of who-you-truly-are. Although this experience is available during sleep too, one is not consciously aware of the true Self during sleep. The state of sleep is meant for rejuvenation.

Even during sleep, when one switches off from the dramas of the waking state, one is pulled into the dreams woven by the subconscious mind. Whatever experiences the mind goes through during the waking state, reappear in various ways in the form of dreams. For instance, if someone could not convince a person during his waking period, the incompleteness presents itself in the form of a dream where one continues to try convincing the person. Thus, the dramas of the waking state take the shape of dreams during sleep.

Therefore, while the pretensions of the mind are going on, it is essential to invest one's time in meditation, so that one can clearly witness with conviction that all these worldly activities are primarily the play of the mind. One can clearly see how the mind plays out various dramas in the process of discharging the roles that one plays. All dramas come to an end upon realization of pure consciousness.

8

Attractions of the Mind and the Homepage

Jay bought a used car. After a month, his friend enquired how the car was performing. Jay replied that all the parts of the car, except for the horn, were producing sound.

This shows that the car wasn't performing at all; it was not fulfilling its purpose. In a car, the horn is meant to produce sound. What is the use if the rest of the parts, some of which are meant to be noiseless, are noisy, except for the horn!

In the same manner, a human being plays several roles in this world to perfection, but not the one for which he is essentially born. This happens because he gets indiscriminately distracted by extreme mental attractions, thoughts and feelings. Due to ignorance and lack of awareness, he indulges in extremes of the world, such as overeating, various addictions such as alcohol or smoking, just to overcome his troublesome emotions.

His only motive behind all this is to get some mental peace by escaping the excessive pressure of his emotions. He does achieve this peace, but it is short lived, at times so momentary that he hardly feels at ease. While he is under the influence of addictions or when he behaves according to the whims of his mind and feels relaxed for some time, he then believes that he is free. Actually he is never 'free'; he has only momentarily quelled a little from the pull of attractions.

The endless cycle of attractions

Why does the mind get drawn into the attractions of the world? Most people consider the temporary happiness or peace that they experience to be their success. In fact, they cannot be termed 'success', rather they are merely a temporary relief enjoyed by the body-mind under the spell of addictions.

This happens because the five senses of the human body crave worldly attractions. The eyes desire to be lost in charming sights, the ears long to listen to melodious music, the nose goes after exotic aromas, the tongue yearns for delectable flavors, and the skin longs for pleasant touch.

How easily does the mind get enamored by the attractions of the senses! Our eyes are our sense for vision and their world revolves around various sights. The Self gets associated with the body and goes after the world of visual enchantments as seen through the channel of the eyes. Due to his fascination for visual attractions, a person thus contemplates: These are the places worth visiting in Japan; I need to go sightseeing in the US; these hills are good picnic spots; The Taj Mahal is magnificent, etc. The problem is not with visiting these places; rather, it lies in the intense addiction of the mind for these places. As a result, the Self, which has associated with the body to experience itself, forgets its original nature.

We also have the world of sounds in which we choose which music to listen to. Some others crave for repeated appreciation from their family and colleagues. Such people are under the illusion that their thirst will be quenched by these appreciative words; however, this never happens. If this were true, then they would have been buried deep in the world of words. One never gets the thought that he is getting sucked in the quicksand of this sensory world and there is no end to it.

Given such a situation, it is only your self-awareness, your quest for wisdom, and love for Truth that can liberate you from these endless and extreme attractions and bondage of the body and mind. No power on earth, other than these, can liberate you.

A man ought to remain awake in this worldly play, and must prepare his mind and body with the required alertness to achieve the ultimate objective of life. He has to unravel the mystery as to why the Self has associated with the body. Otherwise, a person, remaining in an unconscious state, plays several roles and gets drawn into worldly attractions. No sooner is he done with the first attraction, than the second one takes over and this goes on and on.

When we think a little deeper, we will find that from morning till night, most people keeps gravitating from one attraction to another. The mind's natural tendency is to indulge in this vicious cycle of attractions. Awareness helps in overcoming this indulgence. It is only when a person has complete awareness that he can stand apart and witnesses himself beyond the realms of the body and mind.

How should one witness the feelings arising in the mind with awareness? It is a demanding practice to be able to observe the feelings that keep surfacing with wakefulness, without getting involved in them. This is because the Self is so entwined with the body-mind mechanism that it doesn't realize that it is beyond and apart from the body and mind.

While reading a book, or conversing with others, if someone comes across the question, "Who are you", then it might be possible that he would ponder it. "Who am I" is indeed the most auspicious question that can shake the Self out of the dream that it is lost in. However, with most people, the question "Who am I" is immediately followed by other thoughts that overshadow it. Even in those cases, where one actually gets a first-hand experience of the Self beyond the body-mind, they soon identify themselves again with the body and continue living the dream, forgetting this experience.

Human being is so intensely enmeshed with the body-mind mechanism, that it becomes extremely difficult to realize his true nature of conscious presence. When one comes across either a true Guru or some book that shows the right direction, one begins to realize one's essential nature through direct experience. One realizes that the experience of Self-awareness is constantly going on. It has never stopped, or it was never really lost. One need not bring this experience from anywhere outside.

The significance of the human mechanism rests in the fact that the Self can experience itself only through this mechanism. However, due to ignorance and lack of awareness, the obsession with the human mechanism has caused a mass hypnosis. As a result, the common man always remains lost in the illusory world of the body and its sensory attractions.

The importance of the homepage

What should one do to withdraw the mind from the world of senses? The sensory world is just like the world of Internet; as a person goes deep into it, he gets trapped. When you open a webpage on the Internet and click a link, it takes you to another page and so forth. One goes deep into a series of pages and cannot come out. He completely forgets to click the link that will lead him back to the homepage, where he started. Even if some people return to their homepage, they remain confused with the information gathered from subsequent pages.

In the above example, the computer resembles the sense organs; to click a link means to get involved in this world; remaining on the homepage symbolizes coming out of this sensory world; being focused on the homepage means to remain established in one's own Self. When a person reaches his homepage, it means that he has come out of the sensory world. In that state, he only stops getting confused in the world of body and senses. It is that state which holds the possibility for one to embark on the inward journey. However, due to old habits, even after reaching the homepage, out of sheer lack of awareness, one tends to click on some other webpages, leading to be trapped all over again.

This example is an indication of how a person forgets the experience of his true Self and loses himself in worldly matters throughout his life. A common human being always tends to remain entangled in mundane trifles and makes his own life miserable.

SECTION 2

TECHNIQUES TO MASTER THE MIND

9

Training the Restless Mind to Overcome Delusion

A father, accompanied by his son, went to meet the President of a college, where his son was studying. During the conversation, the father told the President, "I want my son to complete his course faster than the schedule. I want him to get his degree at the earliest."

The President said, "For that, he will have to study all the subjects in a crashed schedule. Why does your son want to complete his course in a hurry?" The man answered that his son would be able to save time and start his career earlier.

The President replied, "Yes, it is possible that your son can complete his course in a shorter time; but that will depend upon what you want him to become in future." He further explained, "You see, when God wants to grow a huge oak tree, it takes Him a hundred years to complete the task; whereas only two months are necessary to grow a little creeper. If you want your son to grow up to be a creeper, you may enroll him in a short term crash course. However, if you would like to see your son grow as a gigantic oak tree would, he needs to complete his course in the stipulated duration."

The President's statement made the father see things in the right perspective and he gave up the idea of having his son do the short term course.

This incident shows that if a person has a long term goal, he has to patiently put persistent effort for the entire duration to attain that goal. On the other hand, a short term goal can be quickly achieved with ease.

The power of patience

The significance of the above incident lies in perseverance. In common parlance, patience is misconstrued as a state of passivity and inaction, during which the person has to wait until the present situation changes. This is why patience doesn't attract people as compared to action or reaction. It is all the more difficult for hyperactive people to have patience; for them 'to have patience' is synonymous with asking a hare to run at the speed of a tortoise.

However, the master of one's mind is wealthy in a real sense as he possesses the wealth of patience. For him, the word 'patience' doesn't having a limited meaning, but it is that power which helps a him overcome all kinds of problems.

The master of one's mind lives every moment of his life with the conviction that God has created and orchestrated this world in a splendid manner; people have been bestowed with such beautiful relationships; everything is so magnificent and superb – only the right perspective is needed to identify all the beauty.

When the right perspective gets united with patience, it forms an ocean where the waves of compassion arise. When the breath gets unified with patience, it becomes *pranayama*, giving sound health. When the hands are united with patience, they become the medium for creation of the highest order. When speech gets united with patience, it brings sweetness and harmony in relationships. All these organs are no less a power for the master of the mind, since he knows how to make use of them with patience.

Benefits of the power of patience

In today's world, people look for instant results in every facet of life. They try to accomplish many tasks in a very short period of time. However, the master of the mind always aspires for long term achievements, which are obtained after thorough preparation.

If your preparation is weak and has been made without much patience, know it for sure that the results obtained thereof will also be non-sustainable, just as weak roots cannot support giant trees. When the roots are strong, the tree stands erect on its own without any external support.

The same principle applies to every phase of our lives. There is no shortcut to achieve anything. If your objective is to sustain success for a long period, become a really wealthy person and refrain from adopting shortcuts.

Getting rid of restlessness

A bamboo shoot is the perfect example of patience for the restless mind. When one sows the seed of a bamboo tree, there is no visible result for one year. Even after regularly supplying it with manure, water and all other nutrients, the first sign of life is seen only after a wait of five long years. However, when it starts germinating, it takes only a year to tower to the height of eighty feet.

People find it very astonishing that a bamboo tree can attain such an enormous height in the sixth year. In fact, during the first five years, it strengthens its roots underground. With strong roots, its growth becomes very rapid overground. A bamboo tree has always been a source of inspiration for people who constantly toil with patience.

The above example shows that work done with patience, consistency, and positivity will always produce better results with the passage of time. Those who abandon their tasks halfway in search of immediate results should be inspired from the example of a bamboo tree. One must inculcate these very qualities to know the secrets of the mind.

It is said that good things come to those who are willing to wait. Despite knowing this, the mind can lose its patience during conversations, resort to pessimism, and get trapped in its own world of words. Having patience during conversations can create a strong foundation for relationships.

The best way to get rid of the restlessness of the mind is to teach it the lesson of patience. You may have noticed that mostly a work is marred because of unnecessary haste. Patience is essential to lead an ideal life and to unravel the secrets of developing the mind.

With patience, ask yourself these questions: What are the reasons due to which whatever I long for (familial peace, prosperity, love, balanced life, physical health) do not reach me? Are my thoughts unclear? Am I not prepared to receive them? Are there any wrong tendencies or blockages in my mind? You need to critically introspect upon each of these questions to make your mind steadfast. If you can do this, you would be able to maintain quietude.

Even if a stubborn child manages to get new toys from his parents because of his unyielding nature, he cannot enjoy playing with them to the fullest, though. However, if the child is encouraged to explore playing with a single toy in all its possible variations, then he would derive maximum pleasure out of that game and also enjoy the fruit of patience.

In the same manner, we should also see whether we are able to enjoy the beauty of this human life, which has been gifted to us, to the fullest. We need to consider whether we are enriching our experience every moment by being fully present. If we fail to do so, we would also lead an impatient life, restlessly flipping through TV channels or flicking through social networking websites.

Edison invented electricity as he wished there should be light everywhere. In order to fulfill this objective, he conducted several experiments. He wanted immediate success in producing electricity.

However, he followed the directive of nature to continue with his experiments and understand the various methods by which electricity *cannot* be produced. In the process, Edison devised around ten thousand methods which did *not* produce electricity. Ultimately, he titled his journal as: Methods by which electricity *cannot* be generated.

Today, Edison's wish has been fulfilled; we get light by merely pressing a switch. However, it was possible only after thousands of unsuccessful attempts.

Cure for the restless mind

Can the mind's restlessness be remedied only with patience? Along with patience, the mind also needs the dose of awareness. One can bring about positive changes in one's mental habits when one looks at them from higher awareness.

For instance, a person has the habit of biting his nails very often, due to which not only he, but also people around him are disgusted. If he patiently observes the entire process of nail biting, starting from the time when he takes his finger in his mouth to the time when he brings it out, it is possible that he may soon get rid of his habit.

In the same manner, the habit of watching television for long hours can also be overcome. One has to honestly observe all the physical and mental changes that take place from the time the television remote is picked up till it is placed back. If this process is repeated with patience and sensibility for all kinds of bad habits, they can be easily eliminated.

This applies to 'taste' too. While having his coffee or his meal, suppose a person realizes that the coffee or the food is not tasting as good as the previous day. When his mind begins to complain about the taste, he should immediately ask himself whether being aware and mindful is more important to him than the taste of the food.

When 'being aware and mindful' takes precedence over 'taste', then no food, howsoever delectable or bland, will be able to persuade his mind. It might be possible that others would complain about the taste of the same food. However, he would be able to give an objective feedback with a peaceful and sensible mind, without getting swayed.

Being in the present moment

To quickly get rid of the bad habits of the mind, we need to observe our habits alertly from time to time. Send a message to nature: I want to bring about a positive transformation within me. Know it for certain that with this prayer, nature will also fully support you in altering your habits.

The mind tends to get entangled in trivial incidents. For instance, when a person is not greeted properly when he visits someone, his displeasure is reflected in his behavior. At such a juncture, if he ponders: Is anger more important to me than being aware and mindful, his attitude will change immediately. He will begin to choose to be aware and peaceful.

In this manner, if one critically observes one's thoughts and feelings in a tensed situation, the tension can be released.

There is another experiment that you can perform to keep the mind rooted in the present moment. Whenever you experience tensed or negative emotions, observe your breath as you inhale and exhale. While you do this, your mind automatically gets disconnected from the thoughts and feelings of the past for some time and will return to the present moment.

When your mind does not wander either in the past or future, it stays in the present moment. Train your mind to be in the present moment, so that it can be engaged in developing positive wholesome habits.

Freedom from delusion

Usually, when people are angry, they ask out of desperation, "What do I do now?" It is like a thirsty man asking where he should dig a well to get water. He needs to be told: do not do anything now; you should have dug the well much before you felt thirsty.

Similarly, do not react when you are overpowered by delusion. When you return to your state of normalcy after the deluding situation, do spend time to contemplate: What do I gain by indulging in delusion? What do I get by engaging in negative thoughts and reactions? Is this the purpose of my life? How long will this continue?

After that, you can decide how long you choose to stay under the influence of delusion; if it is for the next six months, so be it. But after that, do not let delusion overpower you, even for a day longer. Likewise, make a plan well in advance. If you have been through such careful thinking, then you will be forewarned and alert when such incidents recur, and can easily tide them over.

On the other hand, while being deluded, if you wonder: What should I do? Should take up this step or that? Then for sure, you would not be able to decide what you should do. This is because your mind is not available in the right state of making decisions at that moment. It is better that you neither take any action, nor resort to inaction, but become a mere witness to what is happening around you and how your mind is playing out in the situation. In the process of such witnessing, you will be able to learn a lot about how your mind behaves.

For example, you can plan well in advance, how to tackle those discussions or gossips at your workplace, which revolve around delusory and negative subjects. You can make up your mind about what you should do, so that people see you as an ideal example and come out of delusion. It may happen that seeing your determination, others will feel they too can emulate you.

When you watch a cricket match on the television, you observe when a batsman hits a boundary or when a player gets out. In the same manner, in this world of delusion, you can observe what is happening within you – what your reactions have been, when you are getting agitated, and when you are overpowered by your instincts. By doing so, you can raise your alertness.

While you practice being alert to the play of your mind, you should also reiterate your goal: What is the final purpose of my life? How much time should I devote to achieve that purpose? Then you would be able to determine the time you need to spend, if at all, in the world of illusion, attractions and entertainment; not more than that. If you have to watch television, then it will be for this specific duration, and not more than that. You would do everything as you've planned earlier, and with awareness.

The grip of illusion tightens on those who lead a life that lacks awareness. With this, the quality of their lives worsens day by day. When you are alert, this degradation will stop and your consciousness will rise, bringing you joy of a different kind – the joy of true freedom from the whims of your own mind!

10

Improving the quality of the mind

Once, a father asked his son, who was addicted to gambling, to give this habit up. He said, "My son, do not gamble. In this game one does not win every day. If one wins one day, then he loses the next day." The son promptly replied, "Ok dad. I will not gamble on days when one loses. I will only play on alternate days."

The boy's reply may sound absurd and ridiculous, but strikingly very often, this is exactly how the human mind interprets what is being said. Like the boy, our mind is adept at twisting the meaning of words and misinterpreting them to suit its own interests. If it were not for such misinterpretations, then the boy would understand the essence of what his father was telling him and work towards getting rid of the habit of gambling.

Creative ways of altering habits

There are various creative methods that can be adopted to get rid of negative habits. If one is truly convinced about the merit of getting rid of such habits, then there is a possibility that the mind would resort to these unique creative ways.

The steps that need to be adopted are as follows:

1. Increase the purity of mind

With the power of your mind, you can do marvels. With heightened self-confidence, you can achieve whatever you aspire for. However, to manage all these effectively, you need to have a pure mind. One develops purity of mind by possessing pious feelings for everybody and rendering unblemished prayers for the wellbeing of everyone.

A mind that nurtures positive thoughts for everybody is a pure and guileless mind. When some powers are attributed to an impure mind, then instead of becoming humble, it becomes arrogant. Therefore, while training the mind, one should give more importance to raising its purity. Initially, it would be difficult to inculcate feelings of compassion and sympathy in one's heart, especially when one instinctively feels negatively about certain people. However, with consistent attempts and patience, one can surely succeed.

2. Engage the mind in selfless service

All the activities that are happening today around the world are impersonal in nature; nothing is personal. Consider that a machine consists of thousands of parts; but all those parts function for the single machine, they do not have any objective of their own. Likewise, all human beings are part of the Creator, and are functioning in this world to enact the Creator's purpose. Rather, it would be apt to say that the Creator expresses through human life. When one is devoid of this knowledge, the mind identifies with an individual persona, due to which it personalizes every activity.

The ignorance of the mind gives rise to the ego that considers itself separate from others, as a result of which all activities assume a personal trait. Given this, if we devote some time in a day, week, or month for the welfare of others without expecting any gain, then the mind will be trained to work without any returns and will also derive immense joy out of it.

3. Remove afflictions of the senses

As our physical bodies are afflicted with several diseases, similarly anger, arrogance, fear, worry, hatred, malice, envy, tension, greed etc. are mental ailments which must be kept at bay to remain mentally fit. The benchmark of mental fitness is somewhat like this. When our eyes see what they ought to see, only then the horses of our wild thoughts would be reined. When our ears listen to what they are supposed to, then we will attain spiritual wellbeing. When our palate tastes what it should, then we will be bestowed with good physical health. When our tongue speaks what it ought to, then our relations will be harmonious. When our touch experiences only that for which we have taken human birth, then we will enjoy celestial bliss. When our mind thinks only that which it should, then we will attain sound mental health and contentment.

4. Inculcate the feeling of devotion

When one develops the feeling of true devotion, he is on his way to freedom from this illusory world. The two main characteristics of true devotion are unconditional love and unflinching faith. Devotion makes one pure and sacred. It is only by following the path of devotion that one's mind becomes unblemished. When we respond to life situations with devotion, it gives joy unparalleled. In fact, when our responses to circumstances are filled with devotion, the ego does not gain anything, and yet, it yields immense joy. Devotion melts the ego, rendering the mind free from desires, leading to the bliss of true freedom.

5. Attune the mind with time

The mind is the root cause of all suffering and sorrow; the same mind could also be the source of happiness too. With most people, the mind generally tries to perform all its tasks at the same time, or else, it does not do anything at all. Let us not get involved in these two extremes and find how all our activities can be set in our schedule.

For example, if ten minutes are to be allotted for meditation, then we need to find a suitable slot in our schedule for the same. In the same way, we need to effectively manage all our activities. If the mind resists too many tasks, we have to get the mind to agree and willingly complete them by assigning tasks in smaller portions. When the mind's working capacity gradually increases, it can undertake more work. In this way, we need to get the mind to work with a fresh approach.

6. Train the mind for written contemplation

Written contemplation is essential to get rid of deficiencies and augment positive qualities. For this to happen, we need to take some time out of our daily schedule for written contemplation. It is the easiest method to give direction to positive thoughts and make a plan of action based on them. Self-introspection, which results from written contemplation, can be an eyeopener and provide one with the way to rectify mistakes committed in the past.

When one simply contemplates mentally, there is a possibility of overlooking certain vital points or getting boggled by one's own misleading thoughts. This does not happen with written contemplation. Therefore, make a list of those habits which have a negative impact on your life; and deeply contemplate in written form on them. Due to this practice of writing, even nature receives positive indications for your life and starts working on fulfilling them.

7. Protect the mind from bad company

We should never claim that we do not get affected by bad company. Only those, who have sincere devotion and love for the truth, can make such a claim. Otherwise, people become exactly as the company they keep.

For instance, a person keeps saying that he always chooses to have soft drinks and not alcohol, when he visits the bar to accompany his friends. However, after some days, you may find the same person also indulging and getting addicted to alcohol. He may then justify this by blaming his life circumstances. But the fact of the matter is that he took to alcohol because of his habit of visiting the bar with his friends. His company eventually dragged him to this peril.

Man gets affected by each and every incident or other person that he comes across. This is why it is said: a man is known by the company he keeps. Bad company destroys one's power of discrimination. Hence it is essential to give up bad company at the earliest and follow the path of truth.

However, very often, it is seen that the mind is afraid of getting rid of bad company. Human beings are generally conscious about their self-image and reputation in society. They wish to safeguard their self-image in the eyes of others so that nobody thinks ill of them. Due to this fear, many a times, in an attempt to secure a consistent self-image and comply with people, one makes a wrong decision of getting involved in bad company.

We must understand that our attempts to project ourselves and safeguard our reputation in people's eyes is an endless journey. The traveler on such a journey never finds contentment till the very end of his life. Therefore, it is better to become alert as early as possible and not to take wrong decisions in order to save one's self-image at the cost of indulging in bad habits. When we become free from the bad habits of our mind, our self-image and reputation in society will automatically improve.

Being vigilant about temptations

What should we understand about the inclinations of the mind? First we need to ascertain the temptations that drive us? What do we get in return that makes us inclined to fulfill our temptations? If someone loves delectable food, he will not be able to hold himself back from the temptation as soon as he gets the aroma of his favorite dish. Others fall prey to temptations in the company of their friends. They take to drinking alcohol to celebrate anything that can be made into an occasion. People also resort to various types of temptations in order to avoid boredom. Gradually, these temptations take the form of negative habits.

We need to clearly understand that our temptations, which initially give us momentary relief, shove our mind into restlessness and turbulence at a later stage. Therefore, one should be vigilant about these temptations well in advance.

Time needed to change a habit

How much time does it take to change our mental habits? If you wish to develop new wholesome habits, work on it consistently for twenty-one days. From the twenty-second day, you will find that the positive changes that you were looking for have been inculcated in your character.

Good wholesome habits never persuade a person to indulge, whereas negative habits and vices constantly tempt and overpower one's conscience. If we want good habits to dawn on us, then we must adopt the scientific method of repeating the same habit without a break for twenty-one days.

While you adopt a new habit, be careful of not discarding the old habit all of a sudden. Otherwise, it may come back to you with double its might. For example, if someone is given to drinking and he gives it up suddenly, then he might soon become restless and succumb to drinking once again. To avoid this, you must advance by taking one positive step at a time.

Unselfish and Happy Creators

Leading an impersonal life is the secret of ultimate happiness. When one keeps an unselfish impersonal vision in life, the possibility of new creation and innovation increases. Only such people can go beyond negative notions and think clearly. They have the capacity to regard everything around them from a new perspective. This quality is developed due to their quest for the ultimate result, for the welfare of all; the motive of bringing 'impersonal benefit' to the whole world. Such people possess magnanimous personality traits.

People of this kind have made a huge difference to the world. They have intensively and ceaselessly worked on the shape, color, utility, nature, and quality of all the objects of this world. As a result, today we see many objects in a different light and their quality has also improved. For example, the buildings, fans, modes of transport, telephones etc. are significantly different from those of yesteryears and their quality has also improved.

These great visionaries, who have achieved extraordinary success in their respective fields of work, were not limited by a closed mind. They had the power to break prevalent notions and challenge old beliefs. They did not allow any preconceived ideas to dominate their thinking They first questioned themselves, and in response made new discoveries.

Today, the world needs such Happy Creators. All the significant discoveries and inventions till date have been effected by such Happy Creators. These discoveries have proved to be so important that life today cannot be imagined without them. Even today, many such new discoveries are needed to heighten the level of human evolution. It could start with any one, provided they work to raise the quality of their mind.

11

The Key to Self-introspection

There are times when many of us do not give due importance to some pertinent issues, and there are other instances when we hurt ourselves unnecessarily by taking certain trivial matters close to our hearts.

But those, who constantly introspect on how they relate to circumstances, are able to convert such hurtful situations into a cause for humor and joy. It helps to have the common sense to distinguish between matters to be taken seriously and matters to be taken lightheartedly. This is because we can never predict how people could react under certain situations. To train the mind to remain stable in interpersonal interactions, we must understand the mind, we must understand how it behaves.

To know your mind, observe the thoughts that arise. It is our thoughts that indicate the nature of our mind. Scrutinize your thoughts by being a mere witness to them. Failing to do so will increase your chances of being stuck in thoughts and becoming prey to them. Instead, we should become the architect of our thoughts. For this, we need to regularly do self-introspection to unravel newer aspects about ourselves.

When the mind is engaged in honest introspection, we gain conviction that we are unhappy solely because of our own ignorance. The first step of self-introspection is the knowledge of our own ignorance. We repose so much faith on the distress caused by our thoughts that we do not easily acknowledge our ignorance. In order to transform the distressed and ignorant mind to a joyful one, self-introspection is a must. Let us understand the process of self-introspection.

The following questions bring to light the various states of our mind. With the help of these questions, we can examine the present state of mind.

1. At this moment, do I have a feeling of anger for myself or for someone else?
2. Does my mind not have any inclination toward any activity right now?
3. Is my mind failing to understand certain things despite repeated attempts?
4. Is my mind flustered and disturbed for no reason?
5. Is my mind hankering for credits and appreciation?
6. Is my mind worried about any threat, fear or damage?
7. Is my mind suffering from guilt or regret at this moment?
8. Is my mind filled with joy and contentment?
9. At this moment, are there any ill-feelings present in my mind, for others?
10. Is my mind consumed by the thought, "Why don't I possess what others have"?

11. Is the thought, "How to do welfare to others" prevailing in my mind?
12. Has laziness taken over me at this moment?

When you do self-introspection in this manner every hour, it will bring you wondrous results. Very soon you would get to know your mind, not intellectually, but through your experience. You would understand that the mind is always in a flux; it can't remain in a steady state for long. Therefore, you cannot reach your ultimate goal with the help of this unsteady mind.

Bringing the mind to light

What would you gather specifically as a result of self-introspection? You would experience a paradigm shift that: if my mind keeps fluctuating so unpredictably, then why should I get attached to it? If my mind keeps getting into a disturbed state, let it be; I am not disturbed as long as I am able to stand apart and watch the mind's exploits.

With this analysis, you would learn the secret of achieving peace without getting swayed by either pleasurable or painful thoughts. At the same time, the understanding, "All the feelings of anger, hatred, guilt, fear etc. are associated with the mind and not with me" – will bring an intrinsic change within you.

If you do such self-introspection with utmost honesty, you will come across this truth – My existence is beyond the vagaries of this mind, and it is always peaceful and indifferently happy. Negative emotions do not have any effect on my happy and peaceful state.

With this understanding, you will be able to remain steadfast, both internally and externally during turbulent circumstances. For example, as the threat of exams serves students to study well, similarly the stress experienced by our body and mind are meant for some higher and noble purpose. Whenever you get troubled by work, tell yourself: This trouble is meant for my mind and body, not for me; it has come to raise the capacity of my body to fulfill a greater cause.

By analyzing in this manner, you would also come to know of your mental state. This however, does not have anything to do with your being good or bad, but indicates your preparedness to honestly introspect. Such introspection will naturally bring about an automatic transformation within you.

The magic of constant probing

How many times do we need to examine the mind daily? It is helpful to scrutinize the mind at least six to eight times a day, whenever you are involved in any activity, either at the workplace or at home. You can set eight alarms on your mobile phone for self-introspection. Whenever the alarm goes off, you can spend few minutes in quiet introspection.

Regular practice of this scrutiny will propel you on the path of inner growth and also awaken the "Self-witness", which is beyond the mind. Awakening the Self-witness is undoubtedly the most potent way to mastering the mind.

Going beyond thoughts

Amidst the pandemonium of thoughts, when you find it difficult to control your mind, then what do you do? Our mind is an endless stream of thoughts. It is not wrong for thoughts to occur, for the human mind is meant for this very purpose. The mind is an instrument to bring forth thoughts, and it successfully performs this activity. All that we ought to do is to give it the right direction and understanding. It means if you are thinking consciously, then it is better to choose thoughts that shed new light on the truth.

When a child throws tantrums and breaks things, if he is asked not to do so, he would continue with his breaking spree with greater zest. However, instead of forbidding him, if he is given another article to break, he would wonder about this sudden change and gradually calm down.

In the same way, if you are thinking consciously, then add another thought to your list; deliberate on "Who is doing all this thinking?" Is the thinker, a thought itself? If it is, then it can be employed to contemplate the truth. In this manner, train your mind with truthful thoughts to make it the architect of thoughts.

In the midst of the array of thoughts that arise, when you ask yourself, "Who is thinking all this?" – your mind can be baffled by this question. As a result of such an enquiry, your mind will either calm down or ignore your question and think something else. But in any case, the direction of your mind will be altered.

So you can make it a practice to ask yourself this question every now and then. It is possible that with such enquiry, you could perhaps experientially realize that you are beyond all these thoughts. This is the possibility of self-introspection.

12

Power of Concentration

Once, a man was annoyed with his son that he did not do any productive work. One day, the son joined a Meditation course. Now the father was glad to learn that his son did not do anything productive, along with so many other people!

This may sound illogical and silly. But the purport of the above example is that the unproductive mind should be directed into productive channels through the process of meditation. The best way to give a positive direction to the mind is by the practice of meditation. Since ancient times till date, many saints and great souls have made several discoveries on the path of meditation.

The aim of concentration

What do we understand by concentration and meditation? The simple meaning of meditation is to do nothing. However, for the mind, it becomes very difficult to do nothing. What is to be done to fall asleep? The simple answer would be – to not do anything, but simply lie on the bed. Otherwise, one will lose sleep in an attempt to get sleep. Sleep comes when effort stops. In the same way, meditation is also a process, in which one is supposed do nothing, merely remain present.

Meditation is not concentration. But concentration is one of the important aspects of meditation. Since the mind cannot be easily concentrated on a single point, it repeatedly throws tantrums. Meditation is the best method to overcome this habit of the mind. The problem of lack of concentration immensely haunts the present younger generation. This also causes them to encounter failures in life. Concentration of the mind is essential to be successful in any walk of life. A concentrated mind alone can bring about marvels in this world.

The wonders of a concentrated mind

What are the benefits of a concentrated mind? As yoga or pranayama are exercises for the physical body, similarly concentration is the exercise for the mind. When the mind is engrossed in too many thoughts, it becomes blunt and gross; such a mind is not sensitive and cannot think deeply. It is necessary that such a mind be trained to concentrate on a specific object to the exclusion of everything else, though such a mind dislikes and resists this training. Concentration is the most effective method to attain stability of mind.

During concentration, the mind is focussed on a certain point, which can then easily get to the depth of any subject. Even in the external world, concentration of the mind is required to achieve anything. A concentrated mind is needed even for studying something. When the mind is concentrated, its memory retention improves and its wanderings decrease. At the same time, the concentrated mind also helps in attaining inner joy that is beyond all thoughts.

The concentrated mind shifts to no-mind state

The practice of concentration of the mind can lead to the following:

1. When the mind is bored, it starts looking for excuses; it feels sleepy. However, when you patiently continue to engage such a mind in concentration, this unsteady mind soon becomes capable of entering a deep meditative state.
2. The mind shifts to the no-mind state with daily practice. The stream of thoughts dissolves and the body and the mind get rejuvenated.
3. The concentrated mind possesses immense power and is capable of fathoming the depth in any activity.

Therefore, you must practice a method of meditation on a daily basis that will increase the power of concentration.

Methods to increase the power of concentration

Let us prepare ourselves to sit in meditation with a composed mind. To get the mind into a concentrated state, we can follow the method described below:

Try to mentally repeat your name silently in reverse. For example, if your name is 'Samir', then close your eyes and repeat the word 'Rimas'. Do it with all the names that you know. Your mind needs to be fully composed and concentrated while doing this exercise. When you practice this on a regular basis, the power of concentration of your mind will increase. This will help you delve deeper into meditation in due course.

In addition, read the following instructions with a composed mind, memorize them, and practice them daily:

1. **Music meditation**

(a) Sit in a meditative posture with your eyes closed and try to listen to the sound of a flute. The sound of the flute is not playing outside, rather it is being played within your mind.

(b) Listen only to the sound of the flute. If you find there are sounds of other musical instruments as well, eliminate those extra sounds from your mind.

(c) During this meditation, press the tips of your thumb and index finger together like a 'press button'. This press button is used like an anchor with which the body signals to the mind. Any combination of fingers can act as a press button. You can get relieved of your tensions any time by the use of such a press button gesture. When you practice this daily, this press button mechanism becomes effective for you. Now, open your eyes.

While you do this exercise, initially you would realize that the sound of the flute occurs to you intermittently and not continuously. This happens because what you listen is not the real sound of the flute; it is just the mind replaying it internally from memory. For those, who have often listened to the flute earlier, it becomes an easy exercise. For others, it may turn out to be a difficult exercise, because either they have seldom listened to the flute, or even if they have, they haven't done it intently.

While meditating in this manner each day, choose to listen to different musical instruments e.g. drums, the piano, the saxophone etc. This will increase the power of your concentration. Try to meditate on the sound of one instrument daily.

2. Arithmetic meditation

(a) Close your eyes and imagine some numbers. Multiply them together and remember the result.

(b) Do this calculation mentally, just as you would have done in written. Do not use any mathematical trick or shortcut.

(c) Keep your eyes closed and imagine two numbers e.g. 47 and 22. Multiply these numbers together.

(d) Open your eyes when you get the result. Verify the result using the written method of calculation. Initially, you may take both identical digits, viz. 2 and 2. It makes the calculation simpler. Later, you may take different digits viz. 2 and 8. Perform different calculations every day.

(e) While practicing this meditation, you would initially notice that the numbers were evading you after some time, which you were then trying to re-capture.

With the help of such mental exercises, you can increase the power of concentration of your mind and make it stronger. This will help you in keeping your mind calm and composed.

Significance of a concentrated mind

What is the importance of these methods for the mind? What were the thoughts that arose in your mind while trying these exercises? After the meditation, you would realize that all other thoughts had simply vanished during the period of meditation. This is the importance of meditation; it holds your mind to the present moment. Otherwise, the mind dwells on thoughts either of the past, or of the future. This form of meditation trains the mind the art of remaining in the present moment. It brings peace and tranquility to the mind. When the mind, which is tired by the whole day's struggle, learns the art of concentration, it will remain fresh and energetic.

Awareness is required in every field of life. No work is possible without awareness. It is the habit of the mind that it remains involved in the external world and gets exhausted; due to paucity of energy it gets drained out very soon. Meditation averts the exhaustion of the mind. The energy that is used up in the external world is reclaimed through the practice of meditation. This energy can be redirected for one's internal development. Meditation is the process of withdrawing the mind from external objects and guiding it inward on the true Self.

13

Getting Rid of Mental Impurities

There was a rich landlord who had three sons. When one of his sons fell ill, the landlord called a doctor to treat him. The doctor visited the landlord and found all the three boys in a big room.

One of the boys was running helter-skelter and climbing atop the table or the cupboard. The second boy was sitting on the bed, playing a Rubik's cube; he was trying to arrange similar colors on each face of the cube. The third boy was lying on the bed with his eyes closed; he was heavily perspiring.

Observing their behavior, one would have thought that the boy lying on the bed must be ill. The other two seemed to be healthy by their external behavior. Surprisingly, the doctor discovered that the boy, who was running impatiently, was actually ill. He found that that the boy, who was lying with his eyes closed, was in fact meditating; it was his natural posture for meditation.

After examining the sick child who was running around, the doctor surmised, "There is no problem with this boy. You only need to give him a refreshing and cleansing bath. He is so restless that he cannot behave like a normal child."

States of the mind

The above example is an analogy that is meant to convey the various states of the mind. Analogies are often used to understand complex matters. Each character in this example is meant to bring out certain aspects of our life. Let us understand them one by one.

The landlord in this analogy represents the Lord of this universe; whom we can address by any name - Self, God, Allah, Consciousness, or Holy Spirit. The Lord is the controller of each and every activity of this world.

The three boys in the example represent three states of the mind. The first boy symbolizes the hyperactive state of the mind. When our mind is untrained, it is normally in a hyperactive, restless and disturbed state, with a conglomeration of myriad thoughts running riot; it creates a ruckus externally. The disturbed mind is prone to the act of comparison and shallow judgments which affects the person both externally and internally.

When we decide to give a positive direction to the restless mind, it ascends to the second state. The mind surrenders to the true Self with right understanding. In the above example, the doctor exemplifies a true guru, who provides the right direction to raise the level consciousness. He brings about the annihilation of the restless mind and onset of peace.

The guru plays an important role in providing the ultimate direction to the mind. Anyone who works on the development of mind feels the need of a guru at some point or the other.

When the need of a guru arises, the guru appears to fulfil this responsibility. Some consider their parents to be the guru, while others treat their teachers as guru, some others consider the image of God to be the guru, while some take the formless essence of God to be the guru.

Only a true guru can teach the art of calming a disturbed mind. The guru teaches how the mind can be transformed into a miracle mind through self-introspection. The guru ultimately guides the mind on the journey of inner silence. A true guru imparts the importance of inner silence and frees the mind from the clutches of limiting tendencies and habits.

A true guru is one to whom you can submit all your ignorance; whose mere presence brings solace to your mind; where your false notions melt away and the wisdom that transcends the mind is revealed. A true guru teaches the disciple how to surrender the mind through the practice of meditation. This opens the gate for annihilation of the ego. There are several other benefits of being in meditation that come as a bonus.

Benefits of meditation

There are several benefits of meditation. However, the benefits that are common to all practitioners are broadly outlined below.

1. **The art of decision making:** Through regular practice of meditation, the mind learns the art of decision making. A correct decision increases self-confidence and serves as a strong foundation for a successful life. Therefore, it is necessary to learn the art of making right decisions at the right time. With regular meditation, we can develop

clarity of mind, thereby making it easy for the mind to make right decisions.

2. **The end of inertness:** Regular practice of meditation brings an end to mental inertness. Due to laziness, people like to indulge in day dreaming instead of introspection. As milk is churned to get clarified butter, in the same manner we can churn our mind to remove its inertness and get the butter in the form of vigor and enthusiasm.

3. **Concentration, memory power and creativity:** The mind attains increased concentration power with regular meditation. Work done with concentration easily attains fulfillment and also brings a good outcome. In addition, it helps in accentuating one's memory power and creativity – one of the most wonderful divine qualities.

    Generation of ideas and solutions, and new creations is possible with the consistent practice of meditation. In fact all such so-called new ideas are not created by anybody personally, but rather, emerge from the true Self.

4. **Increase in working capacity:** When we practice meditation regularly, the mind's capacity to work also increases. If you meditate regularly, you would observe that you used to soon get tired earlier, whereas now, even despite working for long hours, you feel more refreshed and energetic than earlier. This happens because your capacity to work has increased; as a result the quality of your work is also heightened.

5. **The quality of persistence:** Meditation increases the quality of persistence in you. If you start with a regular

activity, but do not continue it, you do not derive any benefit out of it. Since the human mind gets bored very soon by doing the same activity, it tends to leave the activity midway. Actually, persistence is the hallmark of success. Hence, make a resolve today: I will maintain persistence and persevere through all my work, and continue to do so. Above all, be consistent with the practice of meditation. If you act with this resolve, you can achieve huge success.

6. **The art of problem solving:** If you meditate regularly, you would learn to solve your problems effectively. By the understanding you receive during meditation, you would be able to weigh all options with a calm mind during crisis. This helps in finding several possible solutions to any given problem. Regular practice of meditation develops the power of problem solving.

Meditation has a deep impact on the power of listening too. With regular practice of meditation, it may be possible for you to capture those subtle vibrations which cannot otherwise be commonly noticed. In meditatation, you can fathom the depth of your mind, identify the tantrums that your mind throws, and recognize the shortcomings of the mind. Due to inner awakening, you become alert to not repeat these mistakes again.

The example of the boy playing with the Rubik's cube, cited in the analogy at the beginning of this chapter, also represents this aspect. The player attempts to assemble similar colors on the same face of the Rubik's cube. In human life too, effort is made to give single direction to the mind. With a mind trained in meditation, when a person clearly visualizes all the facets of the mind, then the mind advances to the third state.

Practicing meditation

A human being bathes to clean his physical body. However, he completely forgets to cleanse his mind; which is done only through meditation. When one practices meditation with right guidance, the mire of his mind automatically gets eliminated.

When you meditate on your breath, you learn the art of living in the present moment. It is easy to meditate using one's breath as the focal point. The beauty of breath is that it exists in the present moment and is always present with us. The breath represents the current state of our mind. When we are agitated, our breathing is rapid; our anger abates when we observe our breath.

Let us learn a quick method to meditate on the breath. Before you start meditating, set an alarm for 15 minutes. Close your eyes and be seated in a comfortable posture.

1. Concentrate on the movement of breath in your body. At this stage you do not need to control your breath, but only have to observe its movement, being a witness.

2. You would find that the breath is either short or long, deep or shallow. Whatever be its nature is, you only have to watch its movement.

3. After a while, if your mind gets involved in thoughts or distracted from the breath, do not fret, but merely bring your attention back on your breath once again.

4. In this manner, continue meditating on the movement of your breath during the allotted time. Open your eyes once you are done.

After regularly practicing this technique for some days, you may also meditate with your eyes opened, so that when you confront challenging situations in life, you are able to observe your breath and always stay in the present moment.

A human being gets awakened in the third state of the mind. In the above analogy, the third boy symbolizes an awakened mind. He is awakened from within, even if his eyes are closed externally. He has the understanding that the sweat - which was the result of his prior restlessness would automatically dry up during meditation[#]. The drying up of sweat symbolizes the eradication of impurities from the mind.

In this meditative state, the quality of the human mind also changes; it attains divine characteristics, devoid of all anxiety, negativity and restlessness. The touch of inner silence cleanses the mind of all its defilements and renders it pure, unleashing its highest potential, thereby transforming it into a miracle mind.

\# To gain an in-depth practical understanding of meditation – what it is, how to advance in the practice of meditation, the ultimate state of meditation – you may read the book, **"You Are Meditation"** by Sirshree.

SECTION 3

HOW TO BE A MASTER OF YOUR MIND

14

Circumstances and the State of Mind

"I am trying to get you to understand for so long, but you do not pay any heed to me. You always forget the sequence in which these five pens are to be kept on the table. God knows, when you will get some sense!" Jay was scolding his domestic help. He was fed up of giving him the same instructions again and again. His servant was scared of losing his job.

Just then, Jay's wife entered the room; seeing the atmosphere she guessed that their servant had again committed a mistake. At first, she consoled their servant and then pointed out his mistake by calmly explaining the system to be followed in the house. When the servant was pacified, he told her that he had forgotten certain things due to his illness; however, he would remember and follow the instructions henceforth.

The situation being the same, we can see that two people react in different ways due to the difference in their mental states. One was perturbed because of the turn of events, while the other tried to resolve the issue calmly. This is the sign of mastery over the mind, which empowers one to choose the appropriate response for a given situation. With this, one can easily tide over adverse situations.

By studying the biographies of great people, one can understand that they had the common sense required for making progress. They had achieved mastery over three primary aspects of the mind, with the help of which they could march on the road to success. They worked so intently on these fundamental aspects of the mind that these became an integral part of their lives.

Emotional Maturity

The first step to mastery over mind is to learn the art of dealing with your emotions, which can be called Emotional Maturity. Most human beings get carried away by strong emotions and land themselves in a miserable state. This happens because they do not know how to deal with their emotions.

One who has mastered the mind has a clear realization that emotions are actually a form of human strength, which can be leveraged to achieve whatever one desires in life. It is a matter of common sense to channelize our emotions in the right direction after identifying their strength. When we appreciate the constructive role of emotions, we can lead a life without despair, brimming with happiness. We need to strive to raise our Emotional maturity. Mastery of the mind is possible once we learn the art of effectively dealing with our emotions.

Response Selectivity

The second step to mind mastery is to develop the capability of choosing the right responses in any given situation. This can be called Response Selectivity. One who has mastered the mind can easily select the right response even in adverse challenging situations. For example, in an altercation if someone abuses them, they can choose whether to abuse the person in return or respond differently. They can carefully select their words and actions.

Otherwise, most people get swayed by circumstances and react mindlessly, for which they have to repent dearly afterwards. Relationships suffer only because of wrong attitudes and the inability to choose one's response. It is vital to learn the technique of selecting the apt response for any given situation.

When we become consciously aware of how our mind reacts in various situations, we are in a better position to control its impulsive reactions. Every time we regulate the programmed behavior of the mind, we gain mastery over it. Gradually the mind stops reacting compulsively. Reactive living gets transformed into creative living by mastering this art.

No incident in our lives is good or bad per se. It is the attitude that our mind adopts to an incident that makes the incident good or bad. With this understanding, we need to choose the right attitude so that our journey on the road of happiness becomes easy, simple, and comfortable.

Unflinching Faith

The third step to mind mastery is to have unflinching faith. Never lose faith in spite of encountering varied opinions. Instead, with every such instance where the faith can falter, the one who masters the mind strengthens his faith all the more.

Generally, we pin our hope and faith on others. For example, someone recommends wearing a specific kind of gemstone as a lucky stone to get our unfinished work completed. Or they may suggest that we follow a particular religious ritual to get rid of our problems. We comply without raising a doubt. For this reason, many people wear rings on their fingers. Such people place their faith on external factors as a result of which they lack true faith in life itself. They listen to every such advice and keep changing their stance repeatedly.

It is seen that most human beings enjoy gleefully when everything goes hunky-dory. However, as soon as any mishap strikes them in life, their confidence crumbles. Basically, through these mishaps, life wants to shake them out of their slumber. The purpose of these so-called unpleasant happenings is to remind us of the purpose of human life – to gain mastery over the mind and create a miracle mind that can serve the divine purpose of life.

Every knock, every shock that life delivers is meant for us to look within, introspect, and raise our faith in the lofty purpose of making the mind unshakable. Know this for certain that it is worth considering the faith that leads you to true progress in life. On the other hand, believing in hearsay without any reasoning only brings sufferings and failure. Faith on hearsay is no faith at all. With this realization, the mind will learn to remain steadfast on its conviction of the real purpose of life and the grand design behind challenging situations.

True sustainable success comes to those, who can control their emotions, choose their responses and possess unflinching faith. We need to introspect our emotional maturity, response selectivity and level of faith. When we develop conviction in the power of these three aspects of mind mastery, we can develop the ability to easily change the state of mind. Else, the mind will continue to play its pranks in various situations.

Situations and the state of mind

It is not possible to change the situation by being in the very mental state that created it.

This means that a problem cannot be solved by remaining at the same level of consciousness where it was perceived. The first thing required to solve a problem is to raise one's own level of consciousness. In order to bring changes in the external situation, it is paramount to first alter our mental state.

People encounter various problems in life - poverty, lack of skill, ill-health, legal battles, strained relationships, and so on. They spend their entire lives attempting to change such situations; however the situations remain as they are. Despite numerous efforts, the prevailing situations do not change because the state of mind has not changed at all. Therefore, to master your mind, the key is to understand that it is imperative to change your mental state before attempting to alter the external situation.

One has to surpass the present mental state and arrive at the next higher level in order to change it. You need to raise your level of consciousness to be able to witness clearly. With pure witnessing from higher awareness, the problem no longer remains a problem. You begin to witness the lens of beliefs and notions that is distorting your view, causing you to see the situation as a problem.

When you raise your consciousness, the solution emerges from the so-called 'problem' situation itself. With the change of mental state, the floodgate opens for new ideas, help from various quarters, and the problem is solved. If the solution demands action, you will then witness all necessary actions happening through you or whoever else participates.

It is a matter of common sense that with the change of mental state, circumstances also change - but generally people do not subscribe to this. They exert undue pressure on others or shout at them, forcing them to comply. At times, people resort to unfair means to drive their point home, which mostly mars the whole situation instead of making it.

In today's world, everybody tries to make his point stand out from the rest, thus resulting in strained relationships. People think they would become successful and achieve comforts if others comply with them. If certain people obey them, their day is made. With this, they hand over the key to their own happiness to others, and get distraught when their expectations are not met.

If you ever come across any such situation in your life, first and foremost change the state of your mind. Those who master their mind, learn the art of switching their mental state and emerge successfully from the situation. It means your happiness, sorrow, success – everything – depends upon your mental state. Therefore, do the first thing first: do not try to change the world, change the state of your mind.

15

Adopting a Learning Mindset

There are generally two categories of students present in any classroom of a school. The students of the first category put in lot of effort with the sole purpose that their teachers should accord them due recognition. These students work hard so that they are considered 'smart' by their teachers. They pay less heed to actually learn and focus more on being acknowledged and appreciated. As a result, they often do not learn much.

In the same way, there are some people in society who are keen on 'projecting themselves' instead of genuinely 'learning' from life. They are wary of protecting their self-image in the eyes of others. They do not pay heed to whether they have learned, but are only concerned that others must consider them smart or capable.

The other category of students don't bother whether their teachers call them 'smart' or not. They fully concentrate on the topic of learning and delve deep into it. They even take up difficult topics as a challenge. In their attempt to grasp the subject, such students also ask questions to their teachers and may even get ridiculed for not understanding even the simplest of concepts. However, they overlook such insults and instead concentrate on the topic, which is more important to them.

These two categories of students represent two key human mindsets. Let us understand how these mindsets operate.

The Image-centered mindset

Students with the first type of mindset – let's call it the Image-centered mindset – are always concerned with maintaining their self-image. They are of the opinion that an impressive image would fetch them better grades. It does happen sometimes, but not always, because they are only in a race of appearing smart and intelligent.

These students may secure top ranks in school. However, it is not certain whether they would fare well in the same way in life when they grow up. At times, a student securing the fourth, fifth or any lower rank in the class and belonging to the second category of students is practically found to be more successful in life as compared to the toppers in school.

They find it difficult to accept failure, due to the dent that it can cause to their self-image. For the same reason, they are wary of making mistakes or being proved wrong. Even when they grow up, they do not want to be considered stupid, inferior, or a failure.

They are not aware that learning makes them intellectually sharp and provides an exercise for their brains. They never consider that intense effort put during study is actually a mental exercise which is going to pay off in the long run. Few of the topics taught in school are found to be useful later in life; however, the grind that the brain has undergone while studying them all, shapes their lives. For example, the child who has exercised his right hand more, grows up to use its right hand extensively. Same is the case with the left hand.

Due to this mindset, such students waste their precious time in projecting an impressive self-image, rather than acquiring true knowledge. They are unable to master their mind.

The Learning mindset

Some students have the Learning mindset – a willingness to go deep into the subject. Those who take the subject as a challenge, study it thoroughly even if they do not gain any appreciation from their teachers or other compatriots. They are always eager to learn, and become the master of their mind. Those who wish to lead a meaningful life, adopt a learning mindset. Learning never stops. It is a must for every human being to keep learning from life every day.

During the learning phase, one who is conscious about his self-image would hesitate to ask questions, fearing that he would be ridiculed. But a genuine learner does not bother about the disparaging remarks aimed at him by others, because it is better to be called a stupid for asking questions, than remaining a stupid throughout the life by not having asked questions.

It is worth considering whether those students who secure high scores in school become successful in life, or the ones who maintain a learning mindset, even if they secure average scores. One who is willing to learn, contemplates by overcoming pessimism and becomes the master of his mind. In other words, safeguarding one's self-image is not as important as learning and mastering the subject.

Those who have a learning mindset are not afraid of making mistakes. For them, there is no failure in life, because every so-called failure provides them lessons and serves as a springboard to success. Hence, we need to adopt a learning mindset to master the mind and steer our lives to its ultimate purpose.

16

Yoga for the Mind

It is common for many people to commit the same mistakes over and over again. However, those who have the inclination to contemplate, come out with the solution of how to avert those mistakes. They do not like to undergo the unpleasant experience of the same mistake time and again; hence they rectify their mistakes at the earliest.

Every person makes a mistake while driving the vehicle of his life. An important step to mastering the mind is to learn the technique of rectifying repetitive mistakes through contemplation. Some people repeatedly make certain mistakes due to lack of awareness and control over the mind.

For example, many a times, those who are learning to drive a car, floor the accelerator by error instead of applying brakes to control the speed. When the brakes need to be applied, the accelerator is pressed and vice versa. This mistake may keep repeating until one consciously learns how not to repeat it.

Shadowboxing to overcome mistakes

One who has mastered the mind does not repeat the same mistake. He trains himself diligently to rectify the mistake. He gives positive instructions to his mind through the power of visualization. This is also called Shadowboxing. You would have seen boxers practicing their moves alone by themselves. This is a common practice by sportsmen who want to rectify the flaws in their game and excel.

This technique is equally effective not just for sportsmen, but for people of all age groups in all fields of life. If one is unwell, he can visualize his healthy body when he was young in order to regain his health. Through this process of visualization, a person who has taken ill can imagine on a daily basis how he used to run around as a child, or enthusiastically complete all his tasks with a healthy body.

Visualizing these pictures enables his subconscious mind to overcome his present illness. This is because the subconscious mind cannot differentiate between imagination and reality. Though a person may face difficulty in walking due to illness, with the practice of visualization and shadowboxing, his mind starts considering him to be fit and healthy. He soon starts recovering from his illness.

By using this technique, one can get rid of the habit of making repeated mistakes. Shadowboxing is one of the tools of yoga for the mind. To make the job in hand more successful, one needs to reflect on how one can make a given task more effective, efficient and satisfying. For example, in case of communication skills, one can reflect on the positive and encouraging words that one must use to avoid unnecessary confrontation. Everybody should use this technique while applying constructive and positive thoughts to solve problems.

Till flaws are eliminated, we must regularly contemplate on possible improvements. At times, children forget the spellings of difficult words, despite repeating them verbally and writing them down several times. They tend to forget the spellings in a short while. They should be made to use those spellings repeatedly for a longer time. Conscious repetition of action can help in improving it and eliminating mistakes.

Converting shortcomings into blessings

One who has mastered the mind can convert his shortcomings and also that of others into blessings.

For example, when a tailor cuts a piece of cloth wrongly, it does not produce the dress as per the expected style or measurement. Normally, the tailor would be profusely apologetic for this mistake. However, if the tailor knows how to change his mistake into a blessing, he can use this as an opportunity to invent a new design that can set a new trend.

While cooking, if some ingredients are added in the wrong proportion by mistake, then an expert chef does not get hassled, but uses his culinary skills and comes out with a new cuisine altogether. In this way, the mistake turns out to be a blessing in disguise.

People, who are masters of their mind, know this art. This does not mean that you cover up your mistakes or present creative excuses to disown them. This means that the mind can be put to effective use to give a creative twist of innovation.

The state of the mind in any given situation governs the thoughts that arise. For instance, before accomplishing a task, suppose a person considered it to be an insurmountable problem and doubts his capability of accomplishing it. With such thoughts, many people cannot start the work; or even if they do start, they leave it unfinished.

Therefore, whenever the mind resists doing some work, we should question ourselves: How can I convert this situation into a blessing? How can I convert this challenge into an opportunity for growth? Instead of abandoning difficult tasks, we need to inculcate the habit of probing our inner self in the right manner. We ought to explore hard enough to convert our shortcomings into blessings.

Converting blessings into divine grace

Let us understand the art of converting blessings into divine grace with the example of Angulimaal- a dacoit who lived during the times of the Buddha.

Angulimaal was a ferocious dacoit, whose story occurs in the narrative of the Buddha's life. Angulimaal used to kill people, sever their fingers and wear those fingers around his neck in the form of a garland. Travelers, who had to pass through the jungle, were scared of him as he had become a fearsome legend during those times. Whenever Angulimaal was spotted, people would run for cover.

Once, the Buddha was passing through a village on his way to a deep forest. The villagers informed him about Angulimaal and forbade him from going to the forest. However, the exalted One continued to walk towards the forest.

The moment Angulimaal saw the Buddha approaching him from a distance, he ordered him to stop. But he was astonished to see that despite his formidable appearance and command to stop, the Buddha continued to advance towards him in his peaceful demeanor. Angulimaal wondered who this person was, who wished to cross his path without any fear of his wrath. He again thundered, "Halt. If you move any further, I will surely kill you."

Despite Angulimaal's threat, the Buddha maintained his composure. He said calmly, "I have already stopped. However, you are still running the race without respite. Now, it is time for you to stop." His remark left Angulimaal flummoxed.

Then the Buddha asked Angulimaal whether he could get him some leaves from a nearby tree. Angulimaal hacked a twig from a tree without much effort. When he placed the twig in front of the Buddha, he was asked to join the twig back to the tree. Angulimaal was startled at this request and expressed his inability to do so. He further said that nobody can join the twig back on the tree, once it is broken.

The Buddha smiled compassionately, "You have no right to break things that you cannot mend." It was the first time that someone had spoken these lines to Angulimaal. These lines were a blessing for him. He resigned himself at the feet of the Lord, thereby converting this blessing into diving grace.

Thereafter, Angulimaal put all his efforts to convert his fallacies into divine grace. The Buddha guided Angulimaal in his penance for forgiveness. Meeting with the Buddha was a divine opportunity for Angulimaal to awaken. He was completely transformed thereafter.

He had committed countless sins before, and to convert them all into divine grace was a herculean task for him. At times, he had to brave the stones hurled at him by people for his past atrocities. However, he did not give up his internal poise and instead bestowed them with compassion. He thought, 'The bad blood of my body should find its way out through the wounds caused by these stones'. In this way Angulimaal made intense effort to overcome his extreme guilt and remorse.

When Angulimaal realized his mistakes, he would weep; with the flow of his tears and blood he could overcome his guilt. He told his tormentors, "I was also in a state of jealousy and hatred just like you. Now that I am free from that guilt by the Lord's grace, I wish the same for you." Thus Angulimaal sought forgiveness to clear the burden of his wrongdoings and also compassionately forgave even those who were torturing him at that moment. His fallacies and guilt were transformed into blessings and ultimately into divine grace.

His story is an example of how a fearsome dacoit can be transformed into the epitome of compassion and forgiveness. By the practice of intense penance and forgiveness, he could attain the state of Self-realization – the ultimate purpose of human life.

To attain this state, we need to first become the master of our mind; practice the yoga of the mind by learning from repeated mistakes and converting them into blessings. With this, the mind can serve as the medium for those discoveries and miracles that are yet to take place in this world.

17

Emotional Maturity

Our subconscious mind has been designed to automate responses to certain stimuli. Since childhood, we observe and learn certain fixed responses to external stimuli. The subconscious mind is the storehouse of such fixed responses. For example, we don't need conscious interpretation to pull our hand away from fire. The subconscious mind is automatically programmed to respond to the stimulus of fire.

Likewise, there are certain fixed responses that are triggered in various parts of the body from the subconscious mind when it encounters and interprets an input to match a stored response. For example, when we are cornered and threatened, depending on how we have been programmed during childhood, our subconscious may either trigger an emotion of fear or the emotion of anger.

Most people allow destructive emotions like hatred, sorrow, depression, restlessness, bitterness, anger, fear, worry, envy, stress, resistance, and contempt to dwell in them. Negative emotions drain all enthusiasm from the mind and cause depression. People who are afflicted with depression for long periods even give up the will to live. On the other hand, those who are eager and enthusiastic about life, have mastery over their emotions.

Anger and stress create tension in the nerves, leading to pain. Such tension caused by anger can last from three hours to as many as three days. People who are prone to anger and stress even need to be prescribed sleeping pills.

Every emotion seeks attention and release

Every emotion seeks to be understood. Whenever any emotion arises, it is as if the emotion is saying, "Please understand me." Every emotion arises to seek release, to be set free. However, the programming that has happened in the mind since childhood causes a feeling of discomfort. One tries to escape from the emotion, instead of witnessing and understanding what the emotion exactly is.

An emotion is like a child who seeks to be understood by its parents. The child may create a hue and cry to get attention. When parents are unaware of the deeper nuances of dealing with the child's real need, they either silence the child by scolding or stifling it, or provide the child with temporary diversions.

In the same way, man either shuts down the emotion by suppressing it, or finds some temporary way of escaping it by diverting focus to topics like entertainment that provide temporary relief. This does not help in releasing the emotion.

Methods of dealing with emotions

People know of only a few ways to deal with emotions and most of these give only temporary relief. We need to understand the right methods to achieve emotional maturity. Only then is it possible to master the mind. But before talking about the right methods, let us talk about two wrong methods that people usually employ to get rid of negative emotions.

First method: Expressing the emotion at others

The first method commonly adopted by people to deal with their emotions is spewing it out on others. This is a dangerous method, because it has a damaging effect on relationships. Hatred, envy and anger ultimately lead you to burn in the fire of regret. Anger may arise due to any reason, but it always ends in regret and sorrow. The person we dump our negative emotions on, might keep looking for opportunities to bounce back with a befitting answer, or move away from us.

If you feed sugarcane to a sugarcane juicer, the sweetness of the juice is experienced first by the juicer and then by others. Similarly, if you feed stones to the juicer, it is the juicer that gets damaged first. In this analogy, the juicer represents our mind; the sugarcane juice symbolizes positive emotions and stones symbolize negative emotions. You can understand from this analogy that if you shout an insult at someone, he may or may not be affected by it, but the quality of your mind will certainly deteriorate.

If one does injustice to others by expressing emotions of anger or resentment, then he may temporarily feel that he has won over the situation, however at the cost of harmony in his relationships. Others around him become vulnerable to his emotional outbursts.

Second method: Suppressing emotions

The second commonly adopted method is to suppress emotions. Someone who suppresses his feelings may appear calm on the outside, but actually he could be simmering inside. When he can no longer bear his suppressed feelings, he suddenly explodes one day, just like a volcano that erupts when the earth cannot bear the pressure anymore.

If one suppresses the emotion when it is triggered, it makes matters worse. Sustained suppression can have harmful effects of one's mental wellbeing and also physical health. Some people experience mood changes. People are not able to lend the right expression to their feelings when their mood changes. They often keep their feelings subdued. Suppressed feelings lead to various kinds of illnesses.

We need to beware of these two methods. To achieve freedom from negative emotions and achieve mastery over the mind, we can adopt the five methods given below.

Method 1: Take advice from well-wishers

Open out and share your feelings with a trustworthy friend, relative or counsellor. Sharing your negative feelings with someone trustworthy, makes you feel light and relaxed. Sometimes, mere talking is enough to set free many of your negative feelings. The person you open up to, also helps you by listening to you attentively and giving suitable advice.

In the initial journey towards mastering your mind, you can use this method. But you need to move beyond this. You may even write down your feelings. Writing down your feelings has the same effect as sharing them with someone reliable.

Method 2: Encounter your feelings

You can make use of your intellect and encounter your emotions. If you are troubled by fear, take it as a challenge and overturn it. For example, if you are constantly worried whether you might be affected by some disease, encounter this feeling by questioning yourself until you get to the bare facts.

For example:

I have worried about various illnesses in the past. Did all of them happen to me?

No, but some of them did.

Were they as dangerous or severe as I had feared?

Not all, but one or two were.

Was I able to tackle those one or two occasions?

Yes. It means I can tackle them in the future as well.

In this way you can utilize your power of logic to invalidate your emotions. But there is an even better method, the ultimate one, to get rid of negative emotions.

Method 3: Witness the emotions detachedly

The most effective method to become free from the grip of emotions is to view them as a detached witness. Emotions are like storms raging in the ocean. They come and go. Your viewpoint while the storm comes and goes is the most critical aspect of this method.

If you alert yourself and raise your awareness in this time interval, you will learn the trick of detaching yourself from emotions. The trick then is to neither express, nor suppress, but witness emotions from a detached standpoint. Such detached witnessing has three aspects:

1. Understanding

When we observe our emotions, we may initially find it difficult to detach from them, as we are habitually identified with them. There is a deep notion within us which suggests that 'All this is happening with me.'

When we learn to watch the play of emotions from a distance, we gain conviction that we are neither the mind nor the body. The mind and body are expressions of pure consciousness. We are pure consciousness.

When we do not have this understanding, emotions can be so overpowering that we may lose clarity of who we truly are. Attachment to emotions leads to clouding of this understanding. Even to remember that this is "Not with me" can help in detaching from the emotion and connecting with the awareness that is witnessing all this.

The other important truth that we need to be convinced about is the temporary nature of these thoughts and emotions. Who-we-truly-are is permanent. Emotions and thoughts come and go. They are like flares that shoot into the night sky. They appear for some time and then fade away in the sky of consciousness.

This understanding can be deepened by the practice of meditation. When we practice meditation to detach from our thoughts, body sensations, and emotions, we begin to become familiar with the constant background of awareness that is witnessing all of this.

Emotions need to be witnessed with this detached standpoint of vigilant awareness, an undisturbed curiosity with the understanding that it is 'not with me'. Love and acceptance is naturally inherent in such witnessing.

When we resist emotions that arise, we energize them. Witnessing emotions with love and acceptance de-energizes them and leads to their release. Why do emotions get released when witnessed with love? It is because, there is neither attachment, nor aversion in pure love.

2. **Sameness**

The other aspect of detached witnessing is a sense of sameness with which we perceive all emotions and thoughts. Sameness is about ascribing a value of alikeness to both painful and pleasurable emotions. A perspective of evenness where there is neither a like nor a dislike for what is being witnessed.

Superficially, emotions like anger, depression, or resentment will appear to be very heavy and intense. The past programming of the mind triggers an impulsive reaction by giving an exaggerated weight to the emotion. When we slow down and watch the emotion with an attitude of sameness, we are able to question the weight of the emotion. What may appear to be a heavyweight emotion of the order of 50 kilograms will then turn out to be not even 5 grams in reality. This is the revelation that can result out of deep observation with evenness.

3. **Alertness**

    Being vigilant is essential to remain detached. When we are not alert, the natural tendency is to identify with the mind's stories and their associated emotions. We need to have an alert awareness that is uncompromisingly focused on itself.

Method 4: Giving a positive expression to your feelings

No incident is troublesome in itself; it becomes troublesome only when you describe it with negative words. Whenever an incident happens, most people may describe it according to their state of mind at that moment. They choose some words for describing their feeling at that moment, like "I am feeling scared... I am feeling insecure... I am shocked... I am fed up... I am worried... I am depressed... I am very angry... I am feeling so restless..." etc. Thus, they choose certain words for describing each feeling. The irony is that they most often choose negative words.

If you choose the word 'worried' for your feeling, this word will trigger further worry. Hence, don't label the emotions arising in your body. Simply view the tension, muscle contractions, changed vibrations, etc. exactly as they are and tell yourself, "Like every incident, this incident has come to teach me something by presenting me with a challenge. The solution to this problem lies hidden in the problem itself. I need to discover it and use it as a ladder for progress. I will definitely get the fruit of overcoming this challenge."

Method 5: Determine the worth of each incident

Suppose you go to a shop to buy a matchbox and the shopkeeper is selling a matchbox at twice the price. You won't buy it, because the shopkeeper is asking for more than it is worth.

We need to adopt the same approach to deal with life's incidents. If you happen to be upset with a trivial incident, it is likely that you may be paying more than it is worth. For example, suppose you were to get wild at someone when you came to know that he has spoken ill about you. Without validating whether it is true, you may waste your mental energy for a trivial reason.

These five steps to handle emotions[#] will help you get rid of the negative programming within the mind and help develop qualities like self-discipline, courage, power of discrimination of the truth, patience, a flexible intellect, and mental stability. Your mind will be transformed into a miracle mind that brings you wonder, love, joy, peace and health.

To gain an in-depth practical understanding of emotions and how to deal with them, you may read the book, **"Emotional Freedom Through Spiritual Wisdom"** by Sirshree.

18

Maintaining Right Focus

There were two childhood friends who were very close to each other. Even after they grew up, they met regularly and partied together; they used to enjoy each other's company. With the passage of time, both the friends became adults, got married and had families.

After a very long gap, once these friends accidentally bumped into each other in the market. They were obviously quite exhilarated to meet and started cherishing their fond memories. Then they lamented on their being bogged down by domestic and professional responsibilities due to which they couldn't get any time to relax and enjoy the company of each other as they used to before. They then returned home, feeling despondent about how life had turned out for them.

There is a pertinent message in the above example for people with growing age. They mostly lament remembering their younger days and advancing age. One has to understand that even at the cost of a fortune, the bygone era cannot be brought back once again. Therefore, there is no tangible gain that one can achieve by ruminating the old days. This example holds within it a life-saving advice to master one's mind.

Do not lament over the past

Usually with growing age, people start feeling low, recalling their golden times. In such a situation, one should tell the mind that instead of spending energy lamenting over the past, one must focus on what needs to be done at present.

For instance, in the example of the two friends, they used to meet each other every week. However, with growing domestic responsibilities, it was not possible for them to keep up that routine. Therefore, considering their present availability they can form a new schedule. Perhaps, when their children arrange for a party, they could also join in and enjoy.

Do not waste your energy trying to change those things, which cannot be changed.

Let us understand this with an example. How do you react when you or anyone in your family accidentally breaks glassware? Do you get extremely perturbed by the loss and set out to join those glass pieces back? Common sense says that we should do what is practically required in the given moment. You would throw those pieces away in the dustbin so that nobody gets injured.

With this situation in mind, contemplate deeply how you should devote your energy presently. Many people waste their energy in trying to fix broken pieces. They associate a sentimental value to the broken item and think: This piece was gifted to me on my wedding by this particular uncle; I have such fond memories attached to it. Actually, people are more distressed because of the memories associated with the object, than the loss of the object in itself. This is the actual reason for some people to only dwell in the past, clinging to certain objects or incidents. If any object out of the lot, somehow get destroyed, they use their entire energy in trying to mend that.

There are others who ruminate on some unpleasant incidents of the past, expecting some miracle to happen to rectify the wrongdoers. Though they would have already given enough chance to those so-called wrongdoers in the past to mend their ways, they continue to live in the past with the same intention.

Therefore, whenever your mind wants to recoil to some objects, people, incidents, or circumstances of the past, and rectify them, bring the mind back to the present and remind it: Use your energy to transform the present moment for a better future. There is no point wasting your energy in attempting to change something that you cannot.

From Physical strength to Mental strength

How should the mind be brought to the present state? The mind should be cautioned not to focus on unimportant things or things that cannot be changed. Rather, the mind should be trained to strive for what is important for your goal, so that it begins to manifest in your life. Those who master their mind work on this understanding and easily bring their mind to the present moment.

Let us understand this with the help of another example.

When a person with immense physical strength grew up, he could uproot big trees with much ease. However, as he became old, he could not perform such acts any more, which made him sad. This example is only meant to understand the concept.

To master one's own mind, one should first develop mental strength, followed by spiritual strength. Those who have immense mental strength can give the right direction to their mind when it is saddened by thoughts of the past. Instead of uprooting trees, this person can perhaps open a gymnasium and train youngsters.

Contrary to this, how does a common person react under such a situation? He would spend his energy in misdirected efforts. In his attempt to change things that cannot be altered, he would lose his present moment of happiness too. In his strife to mend strained relationships, he would even destroy the healthy ones.

The one who masters his mind knows very well where to focus his energy for his own benefit and for the welfare of others. Otherwise people waste their energies interfering in others' lives in an attempt to change them. They are also ready with various suggestions for others: why don't you do this; do not do that; you are not aware of this; see how I do this; follow my instructions and everything will be alright. The listener would easily get exasperated by these unsolicited suggestions.

Despite this, there are certain people who do not let others use their discretion, but interfere in their lives or blame them unnecessarily. Though their intentions may be good, they do not understand the perspective of the other person. At times, suggestions are provided forthwith, even when they are not solicited.

It is helpful to look within into our own past to learn. If we observe our lives since our childhood days in retrospect, we would invariably realize that we have interfered into the lives of others. There are people, who indulge in the lives of others by way of backbiting. This is also a method of interference. Certain parents do not give their children a chance to learn through their own experiences. They keep preaching in vain and strain their relationships with their children.

The person who has mastered the mind and grown spiritually never interferes in the affairs of others or in the way of divine will. He knows that God plays His role to perfection and He knows which experiences anyone should go through to get elevated in life.

Freedom from the habit of provocation

> Once, a wife asked her husband for five hundred rupees. To that, the husband retorted, "You don't need five hundred rupees. Rather you need some intelligence."
>
> The wife smiled, "Yes. But I can only ask you for something that you already have with you... right?" The husband got the message and both of them had a hearty laugh.

This conversation could have well paved the way for a big fight. Both could have been mad at each other for provoking one another. Those who have mastered their mind tactfully handle such awkward situations with finesse, causing the tension thus created to ease out. Even if a person cannot react in this manner, he can at least maintain his cool, so that the provocation does not have any effect on him.

During a destructive conversation between two people, when the first person gets to know that his words have a negative impact on the other, then he instigates him all the more. This continues till the end of their conversation. At the end, the other person gets affected and becomes distraught by the provocation of the first person. Masters of the mind treat such incidents to be mere training. They do not let the instigator overpower their mind in any way; whereas common people handover the keys of their happiness to their tormentors.

One must remember this important perspective to become a master of one's own mind: While driving the vehicle of life, one should not get provoked by the attitude of other drivers; abusers, and those who overtake you.

Mostly, when people encounter such situations while driving on the road, they react angrily. They allow the other person to exercise their psychological power on them. In such critical moments, one must become the master of one's own mind and not instigate others, but give a peaceful response.

At the same time, we need to remember that the instigators are themselves already irritated by the condition of traffic and that is why they are behaving in this manner. If we also behave in a similar fashion, then we are simply toeing their line. In this way, the chain of irritated people will only keep growing. Therefore, we need to awaken our awareness and maintain our cool.

When a child gets provoked or taunted at school for the first time, he complains to his parents, who then ask the child not to pay any heed to the taunts, lest people would taunt him all the more. Many children do not understand this advice but those who do, stop getting provoked by such taunts.

There is another aspect to this. When certain people discover someone's weakness, they love to touch upon that raw nerve time and again. This is why it is not advisable to discuss one's problems with all and sundry. One must discuss one's problems with only his well-wishers or competent people. Otherwise, people can take advantage of whatever you share and indulge in provocation. When one relates his problems with his well-wishers or competent people, a solution to these problems may be achieved.

19

The Role of Difficulties in Life

A little child wants to play cricket, but has no one to play with. He insists that his father should play with him. The father is not very interested, but loves his child and doesn't want to dishearten him. So he agrees.

The child prefers to bat and improve his batting skill, so that he can be selected for his school team. What does the father do? Of course, he will bowl, so that his darling child can practice batting! Not that he likes to bowl, but he would still do it out of love for his child.

Now, the father would love to see him improve his game and be selected for higher league matches. So what does he do? He bowls bouncers and googlies (deceptive spin bowling) at his child. The child feels let down when he is unable to face the ball effectively and protests that his father is unfair. He even complains that his father does not love him, and hence is making batting difficult for him.

The father then explains to his child lovingly that he is raising the difficulty level of the game, only so that his son can become an expert at the game and hit the ball out of the ground with confidence, without being flustered by googlies or bouncers. He teaches his son to read the bowling carefully so that he can hit the bouncers and googlies for sixes and fours.

When the child learns the art of getting on top of the bowling and batting with poise, prowess and confidence, he feels grateful for his father's contribution in his success.

In the game of cricket, you need someone to bowl to you so that you can bat. Without bowlers, you can never get to bat and you won't be able to mature into an ace batsman.

This metaphorical game of cricket between the father and the child resembles the game of life. The father here represents your relationships – your family, friends, neighbors, colleagues, managers, subordinates, your local civic services and also the government! All these people, who play a variety of roles in your daily life, avail you the opportunity to mature and develop vital qualities like patience, uncompromising love, playfulness, consistency, resilience, creativity, steadfastness, to name a few. It is only when you develop these higher qualities that you truly grow and mature and bring about a transformation within and around you.

When someone helps you in a way that's obvious, you feel that he or she wishes you well. However, when someone puts you down, or constrains your progress, or poses problems in your career, you feel they are being unfair by bowling real-life bouncers and googlies at you.

Consider people around you as partners, as contributors, as co-creators in the journey of your life. Those who arouse contempt within you are actually eligible for your compassion. They may be playing a negative role in your life, only because they are co-creators.

When you catch yourself projecting a negative thought, remember that all thought is creative and ask yourself if that is really what you want to create. Choose to see the negativity that the other person provokes within you as a tool and recognize that as an opportunity. The other person is contributing to co-create positive qualities within you.

Challenges are a doorway to growth

Some of the events or situations you view negatively are actually the results of your higher thoughts for growth, for realizing your innate potential. For example, if you've strongly held the intention to succeed in your career in a short time, you very well may be confronted with a series of challenges for this to happen. However, when you do not connect these challenges with your deep intentions to grow, you would probably view these growing pains and the stress related to them negatively.

In reality, they have appeared because of your higher orders. In this case, they are part of your orders for a rapidly successful career. There are skills, knowledge and experiences you must gain, before you can succeed in your career. Every setback, frustration, challenge, obstacle or struggle, becomes a powerful teacher and an elevating springboard. This understanding will help you entertain only happy thoughts even in the midst of struggle.

The world, as you experience it, is a projection that helps you in your introspection for growth. This is precisely where relationships help by holding a mirror to throw light on what lies in the dark within your mind. They help reflect back to you, what you are holding within the mind. Monitor your thoughts and beliefs, pay attention to their quality, as they are more powerful than you may imagine.

When you find that you are constantly locking horns with someone, it only means that there is some lesson with them that you are refusing to learn. You deny yourself the opportunity to learn by either escaping or confronting the person. With this understanding, you can stop denying and be open to receive life's lessons. Life teaches through experiences that are co-created with people around you.

When do your best qualities get a chance to manifest? When valleys are deep, the hills appear equally high. A blackboard is black so as to highlight the white chalk. When people bowl bouncers at you, you have a chance of scoring runs. The one who wants to master one's mind and become an expert at this game of life doesn't fear the bouncers of setbacks or difficult situations. He knows that these are opportunities to score well in the game of life.

The actual significance of obstacles

Let us consider the game of carom. The game of carom is an interesting one, because the player has to remain confined in a specific area between two lines while playing. He has to operate from the limited space between the two lines and achieve the aim of shooting the coins into the pocket.

Similarly, a human being also has to find solutions to the problems of his life while remaining in limitations. One who has mastered one's mind knows that this so-called limitation is not meant to put fetters around him or aggravate his difficulties. Rather, it is to make him perceive the sense of freedom even within the shackles.

For example, there are several people with physical disabilities, some are blind, while some others are deaf, some are dumb and yet some others are crippled. Despite that, they also enjoy their lives. They serve as an inspiration for others to happily overcome life's challenges.

If you have ever played a video game or a game on the mobile phone, you would know that with each advancing level in the game, the difficulty level also increases. If you have got an expertise in the game, then you won't be defeated at any cost. Similarly, when you consider all your problems to be challenges or mere difficulty levels in the game of life, and raise your capacity to tackle them, then you will happily attain the goal of your life. You will not be disheartened at encountering them.

When you get stuck on the path of your progress, then life poses some problems to shake you up, lest you would prefer to stayput without advancing any further. Obstacles play an important role in your life so that you attain mastery of the mind and continue on the path of progress.

So long you have not mastered your mind, you must not consider your problems as obstacles, but as stepping stones which will help you reach the summit of progress. Actually, we cannot stop obstacles from appearing in our lives, but they can certainly be converted into a medium for progress.

The master of one's mind knows that he has a grander goal in life, therefore he does not lose himself in trifles. A common human being gets flustered when faced with a problem and wonders why it is happening to him. He must treat that problem to be a medium which beckons him to march forward.

Once you get to know the objective of every problem of your life, you would rise to thank them. You would say to yourself, "It is good that I have to face this situation. Had this issue not come to my life, I would never make progress. Bogged down by these impediments, I would have given up praying, contemplating, meditating, following the path of truth and helping others."

The one who has mastered the mind does not consider problems as difficulties or obstacles. Rather, they look upon them as opportunities. Let us understand this with the help of some examples.

- Every day, a person takes a specific route to return home. However, one fine day he finds that the route has been closed for maintenance and starts cursing. The one who has mastered the mind makes this an opportunity for growth and finds an alternative route, which turns out to be shorter and better than the earlier one.

- When a teacher is asked to take up teaching a new subject, it becomes an opportunity for the one who has mastered one's mind. His mind gets a chance to open up and progress while dealing with the new subject. He takes it as a challenge and expresses his hidden talents. He becomes a medium for his own development as well for his students.

- When a doctor is urged to treat a patient using a new line of treatment, then the master of one's mind studies the new branch of medical science and discovers an appropriate remedy for the disease. He augments his knowledge of holistic healing in this process.

- When a housewife has to cook a new dish by following a new recipe, she can use her creativity to prepare such a dish that would suit both – the palate and also health.

- When a student is in the process of mastering his mind, he would not waver even if he meets with failures. He would consider failures as opportunities and work on developing his mind and intellect. He would adopt smart-study by learning time-saving techniques and constructive ways of studying, which he would also use in his life subsequently.

All these examples tell us that every human being faces obstacles and hindrances; however, those who have mastered their mind consider them as opportunities for growth and look for creative ways to overcome them.

20

Freedom from the Prison of the Ego

Those who have attained mastery over the mind work towards achieving spiritual growth. This involves purification of the mind, so that it can be attuned to the true Self. The ten major vices that render the mind impure are: Anger, Attachment, Boredom, Fear, Greed, Hatred, Ill-will, Jealousy, Lust, and Sorrow.

These vices manifest helplessly as a programmed reaction, leading to a life of bondage. Try as much as we may, there come situations when we give in to these negative caustic emotions, which consume us. Every time we manifest these vices, we suffer remorse and frustration.

Spiritual work involves getting rid of all vices such as fear, anger, hatred, lust, etc. By going through the ill-effects of these vices, man learns to consciously choose love, joy, compassion, devotion and peace over these vices in testing situations.

When we choose to respond creatively rather than reactively, it causes a dent to these vices. Such persistent practice weakens the vices of the mind. But this is a slow and arduous process that purifies the mind and annihilates the ego.

Consider a tree that has a big trunk and some branches. The vices like anger, hatred, or greed are the branches of the tree. The ego is the trunk. The vices arise from the ego, just as the branches arise from the tree. Anger, boredom, greed, hatred, lust and sorrow are offshoots of the main ailment – the ego.

Address the Root Cause of Vices

Most prevalent spiritual practices attempt to work on the individual branches; tackle the vices individually. The drawback with this approach is that when one branch is severed, the other branch shows up. When we try to control a particular vice, say anger, another vice overpowers us. This is like a snake with multiple heads. When one head is severed, it raises another ugly head.

In the Indian epic, the Ramayana, Lord Rama tried to kill the demon king, Ravana, by shooting arrows at the ten heads. But every time a head was severed, a new head would replace it. However, when Lord Rama shot the arrow at his navel (the root), the demon-king met his end.

This story is symbolic. Each of the ten heads represents the ten vices. Shooting at the navel implies uprooting the entire tree, instead of trying to cut down individual branches. We need to tackle the root of the tree – the real ego. When the ego comes to an end, all the vices automatically dissolve. They cannot exist without the ego.

The ego is like a shadow, which does not actually have an independent existence. It is the product of a false identity that the real Self has assumed for itself.

Suppose a statue made of salt insists that it wants to measure the depth of the ocean. What will happen? When the salt-statue dives into the water, it will begin to dissolve. It merges into the water and experiences oneness. In the same way, when the ego is made to enquire into the nature of reality and its own nature, it begins to dissolve.

The ego cannot annihilate itself. Can you lift yourself up into the air by holding yourself? No. In the same way, the ego cannot cause its own end. It has to be first transmuted into a positive form. The ego can be transformed into a devotee of the real Self by imparting the right understanding. With the right wisdom, the ego dissolves in the experience of oneness with divinity.

True Ego and False Ego

When we look deeper, we will see that there are two kinds of egos – the true ego, and the false ego. The true ego can be considered as the invisible root of the tree. The false ego is the visible trunk that grows from the root. The true ego gives birth to the false ego. The false ego can be easily recognized as it manifests itself as the vices. Anger, hatred, jealousy are expressions of the false ego. However, the true ego, being very subtle, is not easily grasped. It is hidden and not obvious. To bring down the tree, it is important to tackle the true ego.

The true ego is the subtle feeling that "I am separate from the rest of creation; I am separate from all other beings." The nature of the true ego is separateness. This is not easily discernable. It is the root cause of the illusion.

When the true ego, which is based on the idea of being a separate individual, feels that it is special, it gives birth to the false ego and all the vices. Obstacles like lust, anger, greed, desire, fear, hatred, comparison, and worry may continue to rise in daily life situations. However, the real obstacle is the true ego.

Most people focus on getting rid of the obvious false ego. The true ego goes unnoticed. Even if they are able to quell the false ego for some time, it will rise up again, because the true ego is hideously still alive.

Your true nature is pure consciousness; you are beyond the mind and body. However, when you are not aware of your true nature, you believe that you are a separate individual, limited to this body. The wave assumes that it is separate from the ocean. This is the original sin. Everything else that is popularly regarded as sin is just the cascaded effect of this original sin.

Most spiritual practices deal with methods of eliminating secondary or derived sin – defilements like anger, hatred, fear, anxiety, etc. These are the symptoms of the original sin. Merely working to resolve these symptoms cannot lead to freedom from the ego, as the original sin, the root cause, has not been dealt with. When we receive the understanding of our true nature and abide in it, we put an end to the root cause of all suffering.

How to achieve freedom from the prison of ego?

Let us consider a hypothetical example. A convict filed a petition in the court and worked hard to prove his innocence. After a long legal battle that lasted several years, he won his case.

However, even after he was acquitted, he habitually remained in the prison, happier than before since he had won the case. His friend was also accused and had also filed a petition. But, his friend lost his case. But he was absconding, roaming free in the world.

Which of the two above scenarios would you prefer for yourself? Would you like to stay in the prison for the rest of your life, despite having won the legal case? Or would you like to roam around freely after losing the case? Quite naturally, you would say, "It is far better to lose the litigation and roam around freely outside, than to win and yet stay confined in the prison." However, what would be the reply when this question is associated with human life? How many of us know that we are confined within the prison of the ego?

Several seers and great souls have prescribed various methods to get rid of the ego. The example of a monastic Buddhist disciple will help understand its significance.

> Once, when an old Buddhist monk was asked his age, he surprised people by replying, "I am five years old." He was then asked, "You look very old and seem to be more than seventy years of age. Why do you say that you are only five years old?'
>
> The monk clarified, "Actually I am five years old. I was reborn on the day when I received the Ultimate Truth from Lord Buddha. It has only been five years since then. All the years that this body-mind had lived before that were meaningless. It was no life at all."

The old monk was leading a life of freedom from the ego after receiving wisdom. Like him, every human being has the possibility of receiving the Ultimate Bliss in his life, provided he identifies his false ego and more importantly the true ego at the earliest.

Suppose your friend or relative or your manager at work says something to you that hurts your ego. The ego cannot just dissolve this hurtful feeling. It either retorts when it gets a chance, or keeps grumbling within. Due to the ego, your mind can perhaps remain engaged in pondering how to give a fitting reply to that person and not let you remain at peace.

One fine day, you could find yourself exactly in the same situation that you have been craving for all these days. This happens because without your knowledge, your intense thought became a prayer, that manifested a similar situation. If you lack the right understanding, the ego would entice you to speak the same words that it had pondered and kept reserved for that situation, no matter how your words might spoil your relationship with that person and perhaps cause irreparable damage. Therefore, you ought to get cautioned before giving any ego-based reactions and instead, count the blessings that you have received so far in life.

The human mind always looks out for pretexts to prove to itself that it is special. It even longs for praises that give it the "You are special" feeling. People like to be acknowledged and appreciated. The ego likes to take credit.

What should one do when the mind hesitates to free itself from the clutches of ego?

Spotting the play of the ego and observing it closely is the first step to eliminate it. Throughout the day, from morning till night, you need to observe carefully all the instances when you react from the ego. When you identify the ego, your responses will automatically change.

True happiness of the mind

The ultimate way to master the mind is to give it the experience of true happiness. Without this, it will keep demanding more and more objects of its whims and the cycle keeps going. During the experience of true happiness, you feel that your mind ceases to be! You need to learn the ways to give true happiness to the mind. Only when the mind is truly happy can it give happiness to others.

Understanding of the Truth, True Devotion and Meditation are the three most powerful ways to achieve the highest purpose of life by making your mind truly happy. Ultimately, the mind desires happiness, for which it endlessly hops from one subject to another. By engaging the mind on these three aspects, you can lead your mind to experience true happiness.

Understanding of the Truth

By imbibing the understanding of the truth, one realizes his true nature and real purpose in life. By giving devotion to the mind, it can easily defocus from illusory subjects of the world. In Meditation, one enquires into one's essential nature and silently listens to the song of divine presence.

Without the right understanding, the mind keeps desiring the old and stale. It takes pleasure in temporary relief and by repeatedly resorting to it, gets fixed in a habit of desiring more and more. It forms impressions based on previous experiences and then compares the present with these past impressions. This causes boredom and misery. With the understanding of the truth, the mind begins to stay in the present and allow the inner self to shine forth.

What are people entangled in these days? Let's say there are two categories of people. "All" and "Rest All". All are those who are suffering due to their mind. In All, comes everything. All that remains are Rest All. Rest all are very few and are those who have mastered their mind with the understanding of the truth. These are the real salt of the earth. You may also call them Self-realized souls that have walked on this earth.

You need to follow the Rest All. These are the people who have befriended their mind and achieved everything that they wanted. These are the ones whose life and teachings can direct you to understand and unleash the true Self.

True devotion

After the understanding of the truth, the second way to harness the real power of the mind is that of True devotion. Devotion is the greatest possible gift that one can receive. Devotion is the state of being immersed in the divine love and surrendering all your actions to the divine.

Being absorbed in devotion, the mind happily surrenders and sticks to the right path. It gets happiness even while walking on the path of the truth and feels fulfilled in loving the divine. The essence of devotion satiates all the desires of the mind and it feels pleasant, happy and at ease with the present.

It then understands the higher purpose and becomes ready to surrender itself in love. It is only in true love that one surrenders. One who follows this path, surrenders every action to the divine. It does not leave the ego any opportunity to take credit. It is due to the understanding of the nature of the ego that one surrenders and gives away the attachment with the fruit of the action. By remaining mentally detached from the fruit of action - be it positive or negative - the mind becomes silent. Your actions remain untainted by any desires and brings the ultimate fruit of Self-realization.

Meditation on 'Who am I?'

Infinite waves come and go in the mighty ocean. Millions of them are formed and dispersed every minute. What if one of the waves says, "I am a dry wave"!

Perhaps you might laugh at this statement because you know that the wave is being foolish to say such a thing. A wave is inherently water itself; it is just a part of the same mighty ocean that is giving birth to and absorbing millions of waves every minute.

How can a wave, which is essentially water, be dry? It cannot be. It always was and will always be the part of the ocean. It is the ocean in essence. Then why does the wave say so?

It is because of the upper layer. There is a layer of the wave form, which covers the water. There is a vast expanse of the ocean below this layer and nothing differentiates the wave with the ocean here. But in the upper layer, the wave assumes a separate individual personality and identifies itself as dry. This sense of separateness is the ego.

You need to give your mind the recognition of the Truth. The mind needs to know its nature and you need to know yours. This can be achieved with repeated Self-Inquiry. Self-inquiry involves asking the meditative question – Who am I? With this inner enquiry, you go deeper, understanding the essence of who-you-truly-are.

You need not ask this question to yourself loudly or in words, just keep asking deep within and do not pay heed to all the answers that might bubble up as thoughts or words. Keep asking repeatedly and go deeper to experience your true being. This is one of the most powerful ways to attain freedom from the ego and realize your true nature.

Whenever you face boredom and feel lethargic, you should delve into the source of the mind. The very source of your thoughts. Go deep within your heart and awaken yourself with the power of self-inquiry. You may ask the following questions:

- Who is getting this thought?

- Who is getting bored (or upset, or angry, or afraid)?

- From where exactly are these thoughts arising?

These questions will help you to dive within and reach the source of all thoughts. There, you will experience the stillness of conscious presence. By delving into the expansive experience of your true nature, the mind will dissolve into its source. This is the way to dive into the ocean of consciousness and detach from the experience of being a limited individual wave.

■ ■ ■

You can send your opinion or feedback on this book to :

Tej Gyan Foundation, Pimpri Colony, P. O. Box 25,
Pimpri, Pune – 411017 (Maharashtra), INDIA
email : mail@tejgyan.com

Write for Us

We welcome writers, translators and editors to join our team. If you would like to volunteer, please email us at: englishbooks@tejgyan.org or call : +91 90110 10963 or +91 90110 13207

APPENDIX

About Sirshree

(Symbol of Acceptance)

Sirshree's spiritual quest which began during his childhood, led him on a journey through various schools of thought and meditation practices. His overpowering desire to attain the truth made him relinquish his teaching job. After a long period of contemplation, his spiritual quest culminated in the attainment of the ultimate truth. Sirshree says, **"All paths that lead to the truth begin differently, but end in the same way—with understanding. Understanding is the whole thing. Listening to this understanding is enough to attain the truth."**

Sirshree is the author of several spiritual books. His books have been translated in more than 10 languages and published by leading publishers such as Penguin and Hay House. He is the founder of Tej Gyan Foundation, a not-for-profit organization committed to raising mass consciousness by spreading "Happy Thoughts" with branches in the United States, India, Europe and Asia-Pacific. Sirshree's retreats have transformed the lives of thousands and his teachings have inspired various social initiatives for raising global consciousness.

His works include more than 100 books and 3000 discourses. Various luminaries and celebrities such as His Holiness the Dalai Lama, publishers Mr. Reid Tracy and Ms. Tami Simon and yoga master Dr. B. K. S Iyengar have released Sirshree's books and lauded his work. 'The Source' book series, authored by Sirshree, has sold more than 10 million copies in 5 years. His book *The Warrior's Mirror*, published by Penguin, was featured in the Limca Book of Records for being released on the same day in 11 languages.

Tejgyan... The Road Ahead

What is Tejgyan?

Tejgyan is the existential wisdom of the ultimate truth, which is beyond duality. In today's world, there are people who feel disharmony and are desperately trying to achieve balance in an unpredictable life. Tejgyan helps them in harmonizing with their true nature, the Self, thereby restoring balance in all aspects of their life.

And then there are those who are successful but feel a sense of emptiness or void within. Tejgyan provides them fulfillment and helps them to embark on a journey towards self-realization. There are others who feel lost and are seeking the meaning of life. Tejgyan helps them to realize the true purpose of human life.

All this is possible with Tejgyan due to a very simple reason. The experience of the ultimate truth is always available. The direct experience of this truth is possible provided the right method is known. Tejgyan is that method, that understanding. At Tej Gyan Foundation, Sirshree imparts this understanding through a System for Wisdom – a series of retreats that guides participants step by step

Magic of Awakening Retreat

Magic of Awakening is the flagship self-realization retreat offered by Tej Gyan Foundation The retreat is conducted in two languages – Hindi and English. The teachings of the retreat are non-denominational (secular).

This residential retreat is held for 3-5 days at the foundation's MaNaN Ashram amidst the glory of mountains and the pristine beauty of nature. This ashram is located at the outskirts of the city of Pune in India, and is well connected by air, road and rail. The retreat is also held at other centres of Tej Gyan Foundation across the world.

Participate in the *Magic of Awakening* retreat to attain ageless wisdom through a unique simple 'System for Wisdom' so that you can:

1. Live from pure and still presence allowing the natural qualities of consciousness, viz. peace, love, joy, compassion, abundance and creativity to manifest.

2. Acquire simple tools to use in everyday life which help quieten the chattering mind, revealing your true nature.

3. Get practical techniques to access pure presence at will and connect to the source of all answers (the inner guru).

4. Discover missing links in practices of meditation *(dhyana)*, action *(karma)*, wisdom *(gyana)* and devotion *(bhakti)*.

5. Understand the nature of your body-mind mechanism to attain freedom from tendencies and patterns.

6. Learn practical methods to shift from mind-centred living to consciousness-centred living.

For retreats contact +919921008060 or email: mail@tejgyan.com

A Mini retreat is also conducted, especially for teens (14-17 years) during summer and winter vacations

MaNaN Ashram

Survey No. 43, Sanas Nagar, Nandoshi gaon, Kirkatwadi Phata, Sinhagad Road, Dist. Pune 411024, Maharashtra, India.

About Tej Gyan Foundation

Tej Gyan Foundation (TGF) was established with the mission of creating a highly evolved society through all-round self development of every individual that transforms all the facets of his/her life. It is a non-profit organization founded on the teachings of Sirshree. The foundation has received the ISO certification (ISO 9001:2015) for its system of imparting wisdom. It has centres all across India as well as in other countries. The motto of Tej Gyan Foundation is 'Happy Thoughts'.

TGF is creating a highly evolved society through:

- Tejgyan Programs (Retreats, Courses, Television and Radio Programs, Podcasts)

- Tejgyan Products (Books, Tapes, Audio/Video CDs)

- Tejgyan Projects (Value Education, Women Empowerment, Peace Initiatives)

TGF undertakes projects to elevate the level of consciousness among students, youth, women, senior citizens, teachers, doctors, leaders, organizations, police force, prisoners, etc.

Now you can register online for the following retreats

Maha Aasmani Niwasi Shivir
(5 Days Residential Retreat in Hindi)

Magic of Awakening Retreat
(3 Days Residential Retreat In English)

Mini Maha Aasmani Shivir
3 Days (Residential) Retreat for Teens

www.tejgyan.org

Books can be delivered at your doorstep by registered post or courier. You can request for the same through postal money order or pay by VPP. Please send the money order to either of the following two addresses:

WOW Publishings Pvt. Ltd.

1. Registered Office: E-4, Vaibhav Nagar, Near Tapovan Mandir, Pimpri, Pune 411017.

2. Post Box No. 36, Pimpri Colony Post Office, Pimpri, , Pune 411017

Phone No. : 9011013210 / 9623457873

You can also order your copy at the online store:

www.gethappythoughts.org

*Free Shipping plus 10% Discount on purchases above Rs. 300/-.

For further details contact:

Tejgyan Global Foundation

Registered Office:
Happy Thoughts Building, Vikrant Complex, Near Tapovan Mandir, Pimpri, Pune 411017, Maharashtra, India.
Contact No: 020-27411240, 27412576
Email: mail@tejgyan.com

MaNaN Ashram:
Survey No. 43, Sanas Nagar, Nandoshi gaon, Kirkatwadi Phata, Sinhagad Road, Tal. Haveli, Dist. Pune 411024, Maharashtra, India.
Contact No: 992100 8060.

Hyderabad: 9885558100, **Bangalore:** 9880412588,

Delhi: 9891059875, **Nashik:** 9326967980, **Mumbai:** 9373440985

For accessing our unique 'System for Wisdom' from self-help to self-realization, please follow us on:

	Website	www.tejgyan.org
	Video Channel	www.youtube.com/tejgyan For Q&A videos: http://goo.gl/YA81DQ
	Social networking	www.facebook.com/tejgyan
	Social networking	www.twitter.com/sirshree
	Internet Radio	http://www.tejgyan.org/internetradio.aspx

Online Shopping
www.gethappythoughts.org

Pray for World Peace along with thousands of others at 09:09 a.m. and p.m. every day

www.ingramcontent.com/pod-product-compliance
Lightning Source LLC
LaVergne TN
LVHW041221080526
838199LV00082B/1348